WE NEVER CALLED IT FRISCO

ALSO BY JED PERL

Paris Without End

Gallery Going

Eyewitness

New Art City

Antoine's Alphabet

Magicians and Charlatans

Calder: The Conquest of Time

Calder: The Conquest of Space

Authority and Freedom

WE — NEVER CALLED — IT — FRISCO —

JED PERL

COFFEE HOUSE PRESS

Cover design by John Gall
Book design by Coffee House Press

Coffee House Press books are available to the trade through our primary distributor, Consortium Book Sales & Distribution, cbsd.com or (800) 283-3572. For personal orders, catalogs, or other information, write to info@coffeehousepress.org.

Coffee House Press is a nonprofit literary publishing house. Support from private foundations, corporate giving programs, government programs, and generous individuals helps make the publication of our books possible. We gratefully acknowledge their support in detail in the back of this book.

Library of Congress Control Number: 2026938214

Printed in the United States of America

32 31 30 29 28 27 26 25   1 2 3 4 5 6 7 8

WE NEVER CALLED IT FRISCO

1: DEATH

They say we're a town full of losers. They say we're eccentric, eclectic—marginal. Maybe I'm exaggerating. But when somebody on the East Coast starts talking about a rivalry between New York and San Francisco the truth is they're trying to shaft us. They're saying they're the best. They're snobs. But I suppose we're snobs, too. Here in San Francisco we're proud to be the opposition. We're glad to be living on what New Yorkers regard as the wrong coast, with the wrong publishers, galleries, reputations. We are what we are. And damn the rest of them. Call me old-fashioned, but I'm still flying the flag for the San Francisco Renaissance, all the poetry readings, mimeographed magazines, improvised galleries, experimental films.

Of course, I'm just kidding around here. Sort of kidding around. We weren't—we aren't—against East Coast success. Not really. Consider Mike, with his East Coast awards, still one of us. He's the real deal, though some of his poems, beautiful as they are, are a little too muffled for my taste. I've said that to him—and he's okay with it. He knows I think *Partly Cloudy and Cooler* is a great book. Mike is Indian, Indian from the subcontinent. He's half Indian, to be precise. Father was some kind of import-export guy from Bombay. Met his mother in San Francisco. They went back to India. Then she bailed. Years ago, she appeared at a couple of Mike's readings, around the time his poems were starting to pick up a following. She was much taller than Mike, noisily talking to all Mike's friends, nothing like Mike. Mike, with his sharp features and small, dark hands, is probably at the Silver Spur right now, nursing his glass of vodka, two rocks, no twist. (Years ago I did some bartending.) He has a great head of hair, I'll give him that, thick Indian hair. Still living on the floor of a Victorian in the Haight that he bought a dozen years ago when they were dirt cheap, the down payment from his first Guggenheim. He's very proud of a group of small Rajput paintings, bought from Ray Lewis years ago, when Ray was just starting out, supplying Piranesi etchings of the sights of Rome to Nob Hill decorators but really into Indian miniatures, Islamic calligraphy, and other stuff he just thought was cool. "My Indian heritage," Mike says, only half ironically, about those miniatures with the tiny figures bowing to each other.

Mike reappeared last week. There he was in the late afternoon, sitting at the far end of the bar at the Silver Spur. (I prefer a booth.) I happened to be in SF for a couple of days, printing a broadside for a poetry event in Bolinas. I was happy with the way it was going. I'd started to put it together, using a funky old set of Garamond type, all caps, but a couple of the vowels, the A and the E, were so worn they weren't printing. I substituted a stark sans serif for those letters, and the result was kind of wonderful, the As and Es making a jazzy pattern weaving in and out around the Old World Garamond. Although I'm content and maybe more than content spending most of my time here in Marin, things do get slow. As long as I can avoid rush hour traffic on the Golden Gate Bridge, I enjoy coming into the city to work on an interesting job, maybe hook up with some of the gang, sleep on the daybed in my shop—if it's just for a few days. Anyway, I was taking a break from the Bolinas broadside. I went over to the Silver Spur. Sat with Mike. He'd just spent a week in New York on some sort of awards panel. He made some cryptic remarks about how badly best-selling novelists behave when it comes to distributing money among up-and-coming authors. I'm not sure exactly what he said. He speaks softly, not looking at you when he talks, facing forward on his barstool, elbows resting on the bar, so he's a little hard to hear, even in the late afternoon, before any money's been dropped in the jukebox.

But this isn't about Mike; this is about Marcia, who also had some success back east. Of course Mike and Marcia knew each other. They both went back to Berkeley days. So do I. Marcia, with her dark bangs, was voluptuous or fat, depending on how you saw it. *Zaftig* is probably the word. If I hesitate it's only because the Yiddish sounds a little odd, coming out of my formerly Protestant mouth. I was born a few hours south of here, in Carmel. My dad was an architect who'd trained in London; he'd grown up there but had the wanderlust, so he would say, and found his way to California. Anyway, Marcia was the leader of our college crew. She was bossy, sometimes overbearing, but I wonder if we would've ever had a party if Marcia hadn't said, "Let's have a party!" Mike, although he hung around with us, seemed a little too straight arrow. Always the diplomat. Marcia called him "the ambassador," behind his back. She was catty like a schoolgirl, mean about the people she'd tossed out of the club or at least threatened to dump. Marcia and Mike bonded later, a few years after Berkeley, bored or maybe annoyed by what they regarded as the daydreamers among us. I guess I'm one of the dreamers.

Frankly I'm not always all that clear about the difference between what we were like in college and what we were like a little later—or now, twenty-some-odd years later. Did we think of Marcia as girlish back then, when she actually was a girl? And what of Jack (John to you) Johanson? I wonder if I'm confusing the Jack I knew back then with Jack a few years later. When we were still kids the moustache and the cowboy swagger looked a little camp. Marcia kidded that he'd woken up one morning and decided he was in some old Hollywood Western. I remember her saying that to his face. Now that he's had some paintings hanging at the Museum of Modern Art, I guess people think the moustache—it's developed the slightest touch of gray—looks old masterish. Marcia wouldn't give him an inch. "Those paintings only hung at the Modern for a couple of months, the museum didn't buy anything, so what's the big deal?" Marcia liked to say it was Evelyn, Jack's wife, who was the really talented painter. "Evelyn knew how to let loose," I heard Marcia announce on more than one occasion. Of course Evelyn had stopped painting practically as soon as she met Jack. I wonder how many of her things Marcia ever actually saw. But Marcia had a point to make, not so much to put Evelyn up as to put Jack down.

As for me, I'm not good for much of anything except keeping the old printing press running. I still know how to improvise a new part when an old one breaks down. I've managed to keep my little enterprise more or less moving forward, getting out the magazine, *Velocipede* I call it, a couple of times a year, publishing a few books of somebody else's poems, and then, once or twice, my own. I was just getting the press rolling when Marcia and I were together, a decade out of Berkeley. Since then I've made a living from it—barely. Marcia proofread the very first issue of *Velocipede*. She was terrific, a whiz when it came to straightening out grammatical messes. If we'd stuck together it might not have taken me another eighteen months to publish the second issue. But whatever it was that Marcia and I were up to back then, Marcia was too restless (or relentless) to really settle in with a guy she'd first slept with way back in senior year. I was okay with its being over, although it was a hassle finding a new place to live. I liked her, but she also got on my nerves. Then, flash forward, Marcia was back on our coast after her triumphant five or six years in New York, and suddenly Marcia and I had been shacked up for two years. Or I'd been shacked up with her, it was her house, after all. Her time in New York had come to an end, for reasons I never entirely understood. She could have stayed in Manhattan despite some career disappointments. If she had, I'm convinced she would've done damn well. Instead she chose to come back here and hang out with her old friends—despite all the bellyaching she'd done about San Francisco before she left and continued to do even after her return.

But I guess I should begin at the end, or at least the beginning of the end. Which means San Francisco's War Memorial Opera House, officialdom incarnate, the full treatment: marble, red carpets, polished brass, everything academically symmetrical, twinkle twinkle of bright light refracted off cut crystal. "Oh shit," had been my reaction when Marcia announced that we were going to see yet another farewell tour by Martha Graham, the old bag still dragging around the stage. The piece was called *Cortege of Eagles*. I think she quit dancing later that year. Easy for Marcia to say we should go see Martha Graham. She never learned to drive and expected me to find parking right in front of the Opera House: "You know how I hate to walk," she liked to remind me.

"We've got comps," was her reply to my, "Who wants to see Graham, anyway?" "It'll be a goof," she added, "a goof, Burt." Marcia still got comps, lots of them. Even though she was no longer writing about books, plays, and art exhibitions, there were people who couldn't quite believe it. So the publicists for writers, theaters, and museums kept writing and phoning, even offering to fly her back to New York to see this or that, once or twice mentioning a free trip to Europe. She'd get off the phone and growl at me. Whatever the project, her reaction was the same. "I'm sure it'll be a fiasco. I'm going to hate it. And I don't have the patience for any more hate. Which means I have nothing more to say. I've written the curmudgeon out of myself." There was a lift in her voice as she explained herself to me. "I'm a changed woman," she announced, only half sarcastically. She certainly didn't mind that there were people who figured her career was going to flame up again, with the latest Broadway sensation receiving the full Marcia Lang treatment in *The New Yorker* or who knows where else.

So there I was, coming down the aisle at the Opera House after a quick pre-performance leak, slipping past rows of what back in college we'd called the squares, Pacific Heights professionals left and right, some of them still milling around in the aisles, making it harder to get by. Marcia was way up front, nothing but the best for Marcia. She was standing in the aisle, bent over Virginia Adams. Ginny, her long hair just beginning to turn gray—I think she was a few years older than us, maybe close to fifty—was in a Mexican muumuu, huge African beads hanging off her skinny neck. She was giving Marcia a fixed, concentrated look. Ginny just barely survives on some sad do-gooder part-time job. But the Opera House manager or assistant manager was one of our old Berkeley buddies. Back in 1949 or 1950 he'd directed a Pirandello that he claimed was a West Coast premiere. He gives Ginny a ticket when he can. "Poor Ginny," Marcia whispered to me as the lights were going down, "she has aches and pains in every bone of that undernourished body of hers. She makes me glad I'm overweight. Wow. The old gang's sure all here. They must have been having trouble selling seats, if Ginny got a freebie. Funny. We thought Martha was so important when we were in college, and now everybody's here to watch her fall flat on her face-lifted face. I really could write this up. Do a job on it."

Heavy curtain up; the moaning of sentimental strings; lights rising on some wedges and rectangles of scenery, guys and girls, the guys practically naked save for bits and pieces of neo-Greek getup. Something about gods and heroes, I got that, but I hadn't had a chance to look at the program so couldn't really make out who was who or what was what, aside from knowing that Graham was playing Hecuba and the Trojan War was ending and pretty much everybody was dead. Graham was there alright, an old lady pacing around the stage or sitting on a stool. I suppose the stool was designed by Noguchi, her longtime collaborator. She was rail thin, at least what you could see of her that wasn't covered by a cape of blackest black, her black dyed hair topped by some kind of golden headdress that matched a golden snake winding up her arm. She wasn't doing much, just flailing around with her arms and opening her mouth in what was either a pantomime of a shriek or a laugh, I wasn't sure. I fell into a funk, thinking how much I hate Greek myths and tragedies. For some now incomprehensible reason, I'd enrolled in a semester of Ancient Greek at Berkeley, a nightmare that left me convinced not only that I'd never be able to learn a foreign language but also that I'd never again give a thought to Homer or Sophocles, whose words of wisdom, in pathetic little excerpts, I'd stumbled over in the textbook.

I looked around at our friends, scattered in the front of the orchestra. Ginny seemed mesmerized. Why not? Back in college she had carried around a dog-eared copy of D. H. Lawrence's *The Plumed Serpent*, a book that many years ago I dutifully opened only to conclude that it was mythopoetic crap. Ginny had gotten so carried away with the whole southwestern thing that she ended up living on a Navajo reservation for a couple of years. She's still a sucker for myths and legends, so *Cortege of Eagles*, whatever the hell it was we were watching, was right up her alley. Mike, a couple of seats past her, was dozing. Smart man. A couple of seats away from him was Jack, the moustachioed cowboy now the moustachioed scholar, whispering in Evelyn's ear. This isn't supposed to be about me, but I do wonder why Evelyn never seemed to like me. Still doesn't.

On the rare occasions when I try to talk to her, she looks at me as if I'm something the cat dragged in and dropped on her spotless kitchen floor. What does she have to be so snotty about? Anyway, Evelyn appeared to be listening attentively to Jack, though her eyes remained glued to the stage. Then the applause started. *Cortege of Eagles* was over. What a relief. Evelyn, clapping respectfully, turned to talk to Jack.

"Honey, get me a champagne," were the first words out of Marcia's mouth. "I'll be with the gang." To my skeptical raised eyebrow, indicating the overpriced bar and the crush of people no doubt already there, she responded, "Oh, come on, honey, the tickets were free, we've gotta support the damn Opera House. And get one for Ginny, too, it'll help with whatever it is that's ailing her. She's got a lot of ailments." Off I went, though I do hate fighting the line at a bar. Fight I did, then back I came, pleased with myself to be managing the three glasses, handing them around as I arrived to the rat-a-tat-tat of conversation in the circle around Marcia, everybody more or less hanging onto one of the high little bar tables.

"I saw her in the forties," this was Ginny, "the expression was so pure—it came totally through the body—totally abstract—no mugging, no cheap effects."

"But can a body be pure?" That was Jack, bringing it around to himself. His drawings of nudes sprawled on the daybed in his studio were up in one of the few good galleries in town. Those drawings were still a little shocking. Some of our friends, who'd assumed that abstract art was all that any longer really mattered, were wondering if Jack's nudes were radical or retro or if retro was the new radical.

"Well, Jack, your nudes aren't pure." That was Mike, his face fixed in his customary half smile, so you weren't sure if he was being ironic or not.

"They're certainly not meant to be ironic," Jack returned, professorial, a little heated.

"Anyway," Ginny pursued, ignoring the men, "all the mugging and eye rolling, it's Martha betraying Martha."

"You don't like Greek Kabuki?" Mike pressed her, whether mocking or defending Martha it was hard to know. Or was it Ginny he meant to mock, in his laid-back way?

"Greek Kabuki. Right, Mike. That's it." This was Marcia. She was winding herself up. "You know what? I think I like the new old Martha better than the old new Martha. Wasn't there always something fake about that expressive purity of hers? I mean, give me a break. In her dotage she's let the old thespian dragon who was always in there come out—all the way out. She's crazed, not with the role but the artifice of the role. Sure it's schlock. It's fabulous schlock. Like Sarah Bernhardt on her umpteenth tour, missing a leg or something."

"Oh, Marcia," Ginny jumped in, but then fell silent. So did the rest of us. Not that anybody agreed. But Marcia was beginning to sound like Marcia on the page, Marcia in those essays that both excited and infuriated her readers. And talk about schlock, surely there was something if not exactly schlocky then definitely sensationalist about Marcia's way of eviscerating an artist or an event. Marcia was the higher schlock. Hadn't Jack said that to Evelyn one night? Hadn't Mike said it to Jack? Wasn't Ginny suggesting it right now? There was something carnivalesque about Marcia's intellectual riffs. But Marcia's highhandedness could also be seductive. She was so damn definitive. Now she was looking around, assessing the damage, weighing her effect. Her champagne was nearly empty.

"Burt!" She turned to me with a strange look, grabbing my arm, a smidge of champagne dribbling across her dress as her arm flopped down and the plastic glass tipped over. "I better sit down." She sat, nearly fell backward, onto a banquette, as a woman shoved closer to her husband to make room for Marcia, who was clearly in some kind of distress. And there Marcia was, slumped on the banquette, the plastic glass still gripped in her hand, her eyes rolled back. "Pamela!" It was Mike, turning to the young woman who had been at his side all the time, quiet while we talked. "She's a doctor," he explained. Figured. Mike likes competent women; they're unperturbed when he sends them packing. She ripped open the front of Marcia's dress, revealing a very expensive-looking lace bra. And began pounding. To no avail. Marcia, who some had predicted at the beginning of the 1960s would be the voice of the decade, author of two nonfiction books, *Slummings* and *A Night at the Opera*, dead at forty-five. And, of course, the irony, of the author of *A Night at the Opera* dying at the Opera House, not lost on the people who wrote the obituaries in *The New York Times* and the *San Francisco Chronicle* (where she'd once had a lousy job, so lousy they didn't even mention it).

2: INHERITANCE

You wouldn't have caught me at Marcia's lawyer's office after she died, except that I was waiting to find out who would be throwing me out of the house in Marin—and when. I had no idea what plans she had made. I wasn't sure she'd made any plans. After all, she was only in her forties—so death seemed remote. I vaguely remembered her talking about some distant cousins. Who knew? They might be in the will—if she had one—or they might swoop in and make a claim. Then it occurred to me that Marcia had been fond of Cynthia, whose father, Simon, she'd lived with in New York for a year or maybe longer. I suppose Marcia meant it as a backhanded compliment when she referred to him as Not-so-simple Simon. My hunch was that she'd found Simon a bit of a challenge. However that may be, she had a soft spot for Cynthia. She saw her as somehow victimized by her ne'er-do-well bohemian dad. Once or twice, when Cynthia was getting a nursing degree, Marcia had helped her out, sent a check.

But Cynthia wasn't in the will. It turned out that Marcia had left the whole kit and caboodle to me: her house, money, papers.

Strange. Astonishing. I guess she really liked me. I never knew exactly where I stood with her, but then I'm not sure she knew where she stood with herself. Thinking about it now, I'd say we were pretty well matched, both stalwart but also a little soft and sentimental. Once, in an argument, when I'd accused her of being sentimental about something—I can't remember what—she shot back, "What's wrong with sentiment? Goethe was sentimental. Schiller was sentimental." I had no answer. But enough about that. Somehow I've found myself with a house, a savings account, and a relatively well-known writer's papers, which I've arranged to sell to the University of California at Berkeley, a deal that's taken a year to arrange and netted me a nice hunk of cash; it'll cover *Velocipede* expenses for a good long while. But before the papers go off, I thought I'd put together some of the bits and pieces that I've found in Marcia's study. Do a book. I'm thinking about calling it *Marcia's Remains*. Maybe that's too dark.

Marcia, who could turn out copy like a machine when she put her mind to it, hated writing without a deadline. She had arrived back in California with a contract for a new book, a short one, thirty thousand words about what she described as "San Francisco as she'd known it," extensively illustrated. The idea was a coffee-table book for the intelligentsia, a format she'd already used with some success with her previous book, the account of a multimedia extravaganza mounted in Rome in 1964 that she called *A Night at the Opera*. Her working title for the new project was *We Never Called It Frisco, and Other Stories of My Earlier Years*. On one sheet of paper in her desk I found these lines from Oscar Wilde: "I suppose in about a fortnight we shall be told that he has been seen in San Francisco. It is an odd thing, but every one who disappears is said to be seen at San Francisco. It must be a delightful city, and possess all the attractions of the next world." Below this typewritten couple of sentences, in Marcia's rather small, tight handwriting, there's this: "Maybe an epigraph?"

Marcia didn't talk about the new book, at least not to me, except to sometimes wonder if she'd ever manage to finish. She'd come down from her study and tell me that she'd just torn up some account of an old friend, disgusted with the damn thing. She said that so-and-so's trials and tribulations were too silly to hold up on the page. I think the truth was that she didn't know what she thought about the San Francisco scene she'd fled in 1958. Back then she'd been annoyed by what she described as the provincial pretensions of her artist and poet friends. Now, nearly a decade later, she found herself thinking about what she'd liked about life in North Beach—and wondering where we were all headed. She was infuriated by everything about the Summer of Love. (And to think that was her last summer.) She had no patience with what she called the "stupid bliss" of the Haight-Ashbury scene. Luckily, she wasn't publishing at that point. If she'd said anything like that in print, the younger generation would've dismissed her as an old fart. I wouldn't have wanted to be around to hear her reactions to *that*. In a way she was an old fart—an old soul. She may have believed she was defending the best of bohemia against the commercialization of bohemia—although she never quite came out and said that.

I can't say I was surprised the morning Marcia's obit appeared in the *Times*, when her editor, Sandra Stone, called from New York. I hadn't spoken to her before and my impression was that Marcia herself hadn't talked with her much. She'd pretty much taken the money and run. Stone was full of condolences and questions. It was a disorganized phone call. She didn't seem to know where to begin. I sometimes wonder if editors, when they're acting all confused, are really just trying to throw the writer off-balance—soften the author up before making a lowball offer on the next project or breaking the news that the current manuscript needs a total rewrite. Stone eventually got around to asking whether Marcia had made much headway with the book. I told her I wasn't sure what there was in Marcia's study. I invited her to come out and take a look. A week later Sandra Stone appeared and spent an afternoon here in Marin. Her conclusion was that whatever there was wasn't enough for a book, at least not a book that a New York trade publisher could put out. She didn't seem surprised. "It happens more often than you'd think, or we'd care to admit," was her comment as she got back in the rental car. As for the advance? I think I get to keep it. So whatever bits and pieces Marcia managed to produce when she was up in her study are going into this little book, along with the letters a few friends have let me have.

It turns out that Ginny, of all people, had a pile of them. The letters arrived at my place in a manila folder, most of them still in their original envelopes. They came with a note in Ginny's clear cursive handwriting, which probably hasn't changed since elementary school:

Dear Burt,

Here are Marcia's letters, which I promised you. I was planning to have copies made and keep the originals. But then I decided it just wasn't worth the hassle and expense of going to the copy shop. I'm really living on a shoestring, you know. So here are the originals. They're yours. What do I need them for, anyway? I never really understood why Marcia wrote to me. What did she think she was proving? Just rubbing my face in the fact that while she paraded around New York and Rome I was still back in SF working at crummy do-gooder jobs? She always said she loved me. It was always, "Oh, Ginny, you've stuck to your guns, you've stood your ground!" Which left me thinking she had no idea what ground I was standing on. Even that last night, at the Opera House, it was "Oh, Ginny, so great to see you!" Frankly, I never liked her. She was a showboat in college and a worse showboat after that. That magazine she wrote for, what was it called? *Spectacles*. That's perfect. Beyond perfect. Anyway, weren't most of the artists and performances she wrote about garbage? She had her clever way of spinning it. But nothing she did really mattered. Of course what does anything any of us do really matter? Burt, I'm sorry to go off on you like this. I know you really liked her. Did you actually love her? What a ridiculous question. Forget it. The letters are yours. I guess if you try to sell them (would anybody want them?) it would be nice if you gave some of the proceeds to charity. But that's up to you. Sincerely, Ginny

So here I am, sitting in the house in Marin with Marcia's miscellaneous stuff, wondering exactly what she was up to with *We Never Called It Frisco*. Just now I was thinking about how she liked to skewer our friends on the drives back from parties in San Francisco. She had this theory that our friends, "The whole *La Bohème* gang," as she put it, were parasites. Did she really believe it? I think she was trying something out, a nifty idea for an essay. Marcia specialized in impressions, not facts. Bohemia, she liked to say, cannibalized older communities and cultures. "Bohemia isn't avant-garde," she announced, "it's retrograde, fundamentally conservative. Consider Picasso and his poet buddies before World War I, obsessed with the faded leftovers of the nineteenth-century circus, or reciting Villon's poetry as they wandered around late night Paris, imagining it was fourteenth-century Paris—or whatever century it was Villon lived." Marcia didn't think she was offending our cohort when she accused them of being conservatives. She was doing them a favor, telling them the truth—as she saw it. Or maybe she just enjoyed knowing that she was up to no good. Of course, as I've already said, Marcia herself could be nostalgic, with a soft spot for gauzy theatrical performances and the antique dolls and dollhouse accessories she picked up, always at bargain prices, or so she said, at flea markets here and there. When challenged about her romanticism she would cheerfully admit to having a sentimental side. "You can't be a total hard-ass if you're going to care about the arts. At least not if you're going to enjoy anything but Kafka and Beckett—and they bore me to tears." But she could be scathing when it came to anybody else's soft side. She worried that romanticism was all too often an excuse for complacency.

The North Beach neighborhood where we had all started out, so Marcia said, was the old Italian North Beach, only neutered by a bohemian tendency to romanticize everything. In her view our San Francisco scene was make-believe, a wraparound theatrical production. She believed we liked it that way—even she liked it that way, at least some of the time. But exactly what way was that? I remember one male artist backing away from Marcia when she suggested that he and his artist and writer friends (they were her friends, too) had neutered North Beach. He later told me how uncomfortable he'd felt, as if Marcia, who was in one of her more vehement moods, were holding a knife a little too close to his crotch. Instead of making shoes, bread, or sausages, something useful, our friends made paintings and poems, so Marcia liked to say. Was this necessarily a bad thing? She never really explained herself. Once, confronted by a Marxist at a party, she announced, "Abstract art is an abstraction of work." Did she believe it? And what did it mean, anyway? It hardly mattered. She liked some of the artists. She was offering a backhanded compliment, saying guys would be guys, when she announced that all that was left of the purposefulness of work was "an old-fashioned masculine grace." "I like the theatricality," she acknowledged. "But everybody's playing the same old roles—and not playing them very well. I enjoy the swagger. But what's the plot?" She pointed out that some of her artist friends made their work in the same old spaces, the bakery or shoe repair shop now a studio, the windows painted black so they wouldn't be bothered by pedestrians. "There goes the neighborhood," she said, "from reality to fantasy." When asked what she meant she shot back, "It depends on how you define fantasy."

When Marcia made her arguments at parties, I could see people thinking she was just being perverse, though very few of our friends were willing to call her bluff. Her ideas were scattershot—a fusillade of observations, conjectures, and pronouncements. Anyway, what was she if not one of us? Maybe that's why her skepticism about the San Francisco avant-garde was tossed off with a dash of optimism, what I once heard her refer to as "provincialism plus." "Don't feel left out," she'd say. "Find a different way out." She thought the relationship between Broadway and regional theater offered an analogy. "Sometimes," she said, "the theater companies in smaller cities try things the big New York outfits are too ossified or afraid to touch. Study the story of the tortoise and the hare." Marcia predicted that what a scholar she referred to as "a pedant," I think she was citing the English art historian Kenneth Clark, had called "the struggle with the dominant style," whether in painting or in poetry, would eventually generate a triumphantly idiosyncratic style, although she hastened to add that she hadn't seen it yet. "There's a difference between slow and steady and slowpoke," she whispered to me during a particularly dreary evening of short films by a local experimentalist I would prefer not to name. He believed Marcia liked him—she did—so there's no point in hurting his feelings now that she's gone.

We were supposed to be contrarians. But not everybody could stomach Marcia's cheerful combat. To some it felt like out and out hostility. She certainly wasn't very good at knowing who could and who couldn't tolerate her attacks. There were evenings when she was so combative that I wondered if we'd be invited back. Maybe she didn't care. Anyway, she knew from experience that she would be invited back. People couldn't resist finding out what she'd say next. "Collage," I once heard her announce, "the ultimate avant garde art act, is just cannibalism." Joseph Cornell, she said, was "a sentimental cannibal." I still remember the pained expression on a kindhearted painter's face as he listened to Marcia skewer his favorite artist. "But the poetry of those boxes!" he meekly responded. She wouldn't deign to reply. "Look at you, Burt," she once said when it was just the two of us, "publishing your little poetry books on a press you got for free from a printer who was going out of business, retiring to Florida, something like that. Hadn't he done work for a bunch of Bay Area drugstores? And what do you do? Poetry. And those typefaces and fancy initials and decorations of yours that everybody thinks are cool? Didn't you find a lot of that stuff in dumpsters?"

Did it occur to Marcia that I might be insulted—or, as she would put it, take it the wrong way? I wasn't sure. I'm still not sure. She was so immune to hurt, so good at bouncing back, that she couldn't very easily conceive of other people's wounded feelings. At least that was true until her early successes in New York failed to produce the long-term professional security she had surely believed she deserved. Of course I've never really understood why she turned her back on New York after doing so well there. I suppose I could have pressed her on that. But I've never been much for conversational repartee—or asking the kind of questions that demand an uncomfortable answer. At times Marcia complained that I didn't say enough. She called me, heavy with irony, "The silent one." That left her free to proceed. "There's a bit of a bottom feeder in every bohemian," she announced after accusing me of commandeering a printing press and a bunch of type that somebody else had abandoned. I really didn't see what was wrong with that. "Maybe," I said in response. That was all I said. To which Marcia, heading to the kitchen with the dirty dishes, called back, "Maybe baby!"

I have a feeling that Marcia wouldn't approve of what I'm doing with what's left of her writing, turning the work of this woman who hated collage into a collage of a book. Not long before she died, when Robert Duncan (his arrogance amused Marcia) announced at a party that Pindar was great because he made mosaics, not pillars, she shot back that that was "fragment fetishism." "Get over it, Robert. And while you're at it, get over Pound." *The Cantos*, she pursued, was a boondoggle, nothing more. But Marcia, who was always shaming modernism or what she said were the delusions of modernism, couldn't do without it. (I'd once heard her fondly quote Pound's "What thou lovest well remains . . . ," from Canto LXXXI.) One critic, reviewing *Slummings*, the essay collection that put her on the map in New York in 1963, got it right when he said she was "the hipster's conservative." The secret of her brief years of success in New York, at least part of the secret, was that the readers who looked to her to tell them what was hot and hip were relieved to find her skewering the stuff they wouldn't have known about if she hadn't written about it in the first place. First she informed. Then she gave her readers permission to reject that information. If she'd been a Biblical character, the King James Version would have summed her up thus: "Marcia Lang giveth and Marcia Lang taketh away."

As for me, she pissed me off some but mostly I admired her. There's love in her hate. Going through all her stuff now—I hadn't really looked at *Slummings* since it came out six or seven years ago—I think she spoke for the mixed emotions of a lot of our gang, the sneaking suspicion that there's something comic if not slightly ridiculous about the way we live. Most of what she was writing for her new book was fairly personal. That surprised me. It may have worried her. Was she afraid of exposing her softer side? I even make an appearance or two. I'm not sure what her plans were. Was she going to begin with something retrospective, a little piece about San Francisco around 1900? I've decided that it's more fun to begin with one of her crushes. I've sort of scrambled the chronology. Every chapter or two I've added a chapter that's more or less my own—to fill in the gaps in the story, I guess. Mike has read some of the pages I've written. He says I sound an awful lot like Marcia and wonders if that's a problem. Maybe it is. But I can't help it. I'm a bit of a sponge. I have a passive side. During the years we were together I did a lot of listening while she did a lot of talking. I guess I've assimilated her verbal tricks and turns of phrase. Maybe it's just as well that the whole book sounds like Marcia. As for what kind of book it is, I'm reminded of something William Carlos Williams says at the beginning of *The Great American Novel*: "If there is progress then there is a novel." Maybe this is a novel. I wonder what Marcia would've thought. She might have hated this collage of a book. Or maybe not. I don't care. I'm glad I've done it.

3: THE PHOTOGRAPHER

He was still tall, easy on his feet, an elegant wreck of a man. Cal Cummings, photographer, nearly forgotten when I knew him. Nobody gave a damn about photography then. Photography was *Life* magazine clichés and sentimentalities. Unless it was abstract—that we could accept—a close-up of a battered stretch of wall by Aaron Siskind or a study of some weeds by Harry Callahan. As for Cal Cummings, he was old-school, old hat. He certainly wasn't somebody it would have occurred to me to take an interest in, at least not when I was thirty. I hadn't even heard of him until I got the assignment from the *Chronicle*, one of the pathetic gigs they gave me during the miserable years I worked there.

But once I got to know him I liked him. I remember him at one of my parties, an enigma of a man somehow mixed up with our gang. Bearded, gray-haired, the skin weather-beaten, he was an El Greco saint with blue eyes undimmed. He wore tattered tweed jackets and wool slacks, not exactly clean. He smelled of the garlic that he ate at most meals and believed would keep him alive until kingdom come. "Kingdom come" was his phrase, not mine. When you talked with Cal, you were talking with another San Francisco—an earlier one. It wasn't clear how he'd ended up in the Bay Area, which I eventually gathered was sometime in the 1930s. He told his story in dribs and drabs. I wasn't the best listener, too involved with the impression I was making to take much of an interest. He had been touring as a dancer, associated in some way, he was never clear about it, with Ruth St. Denis or maybe Ted Shawn or maybe it was just a circus or vaudeville act. I've seen a lot of modern dance but I'm fairly hazy when it comes to the history. I imagined him in a costume that looked like baggy pajamas, pulling and pushing a girl around the stage, angular movements timed to Beethoven or Chopin. About that I may be completely wrong. My guess is that he was striking to look at but not a very good dancer, which might explain why he resigned or was fired from whatever company it was when they reached San Francisco.

The *San Francisco Chronicle* had a feature, "Old San Francisco," a picture and a couple of nostalgic columns on a place, person, or thing. Cal was perfect. The few people at the *Chronicle* who'd even given a thought to him had assumed he was dead. As I said, I hadn't even heard of him. Then somebody at the paper ran into an old guy at a party who turned out to be Cal Cummings. Of course he wasn't that ancient, maybe sixty-five, he just seemed old to us. A few of his photographs of Chinatown in the 1930s were reprinted in books and magazines fairly frequently, whenever authors or editors wanted a glimpse of San Francisco before the tourists and the corporations took over. You've seen those photographs, with the adorable little

Chinese children in traditional outfits and the old men with their wispy beards peering into the camera as if they were about to offer the wisdom of the ages. When I checked out the photographs I found them sloppy and gimmicky, too many blurred edges and misty backgrounds. But it was an assignment. It turned out that Cal was still living where he'd been for decades, upstairs in the building owned by Sing Fat Co., the Chinese emporium on the corner of California and Grant. Sing Fat was where friends went to buy a Christmas present for a mother or an aunt in the Midwest, an embroidered robe, a porcelain tea pot, a Mahjong set. For more adventuresome relatives there were elaborate silk or paper lanterns and kites shaped like animals. The whole building smelled of incense, strong tea, and decades of dust. A curator once told me that somewhere in the bowels of the place there were still twelfth-century statues of the Buddha, outrageously rare, priced sky high.

"You don't really like my Chinatown pictures, do you?" Cal asked me after the little piece that I'd written came out in the *Chronicle*. I was embarrassed by the question. I realized that he'd seen through my mildly enthusiastic remarks, when all the while I'd imagined that I had him wrapped around my little finger, a good-looking girl knocking on the door with the stained business card thumbtacked to it: "Cal Cummings—Art Photography—San Francisco." I had mistaken his courtliness for a lack of insight. I was caught out in thinking his work saccharine. "Oh no, the photograph we reproduced, I thought that was gorgeous." But of course that was as much as admitting that I didn't like the others. I'm not sure he cared. He kept his own counsel. "Let me show you some things that hardly anybody has ever seen." He had an old cardboard box on the table where we were sitting, drinking a glass of wine. He moved the bottle and the glasses off the table. Quickly but carefully, as if shuffling cards or preparing a magic trick, he set before me a dozen photographs, the hazy grays of some ancient photographic process, platinum or palladium a friend tells me it must have been, mounted on heavy card stock. There were two figures in each photograph, a man and a woman, buck naked in the woods, I thought maybe it was Muir Woods. Sometimes the man was crouching and the woman turning away, sometimes it was the other way around. For a moment I thought it was just Symbolist hokum, but the figures were too real for that. You could almost feel them shivering as they turned themselves into icons or idols or I don't know what. "Is that you?" I asked, looking at one photograph of a tall, slim man on his knees, head bent, one arm reaching toward the woman as she turned away from him, or maybe just averted her eyes from his. Cal didn't give me an answer. He just raised an eyebrow as he put the photographs back in the box. Of course it was him.

It was such an old-time seduction. Come up and see my photographs. I was flattered, arrogant. We never made it, at least not exactly. Feeling awkward, I aimed to be glib. I tossed off a cliché. "You're old enough to be my grandfather." To which he responded, "Oh, well." I felt so much wiser than Cal, with his hazy shots of Chinatown and his old-fashioned erotica. But there I was, semi-seduced. He saw through me. He was too much the gentleman to tell me that I was inhibited, afraid that I'd enjoy having a handsome man kneeling at my feet. He took me as I was. He took me in stride. He sat up in bed, wearing the undershirt that he never seemed to want to take off, smoking a cigarette, the strong smell of his Camel mixed with the garlic and the photographic chemicals in his darkroom next door. The way he looked at me was the damnedest combination of affectionate and take-it-or-leave-it. I took it. I left it.

4: PARTY

"You'll make sure the drinks don't run out, okay?" How could I say no to Marcia? Little did I know it was the last party we'd share in her North Beach apartment. Frankly, I don't think she knew either. I could see she was feeling restless. She was picking little fights with me. Marcia was in the midst of her job at the *San Francisco Chronicle*. Determined, bulldozer Marcia. Every morning she marched off to her job as a typist at the *Chronicle*, the only job remotely journalistic she could get. "It's not a typing pool," she would say. "It's a typing puddle." When she was really demoralized it was "a typing sewer." It didn't matter how late she'd been up defending Cocteau or Tennessee Williams in an argument with friends around the old round oak table—Marcia's opinions about theater were already fixed—the next morning she was awake before her alarm, gearing up for the day. "See you later, lazybones!" was her exit line. I was still in bed, trying to remember which part-time job I was due at that afternoon.

I don't think she particularly cared that I didn't have any regular employment. She was all for my plan to run a little press. She said a couple of my poems weren't half bad. But she worried that I wasn't doing enough about any of it. She worried that I wasn't ambitious. She never said it. I think she thought it. Maybe I'm wrong. Anyway, she wasn't entirely wrong. I'm not that ambitious. Or she might have just been thinking about herself, her own ambitions. We had our arguments. But I can't really remember how the arguments went. Maybe we were just letting off steam. Maybe I'm making it all sound more confusing than it was. We had a lot of good times. That's the main thing. Warm winter Saturdays, we'd take a salami, a loaf of bread, and a bottle of wine and walk the blocks to the Palace of Fine Arts, the lone ruin left from the 1915 Panama-Pacific International Exposition, crawl through a break in the chain-link fence and sit amid the decrepit magnificence. "A masterpiece of California classicism," Marcia would explain to our friends. "Bernard Maybeck, who designed it, made the columns as massive as redwood trees." She scrounged for volutes and curlicues that had fallen off the crumbling plaster Corinthian columns. She took them home and lined them up on a windowsill.

Marcia's apartment was big, bright, and generally pretty nifty, even if there were problems with the plumbing, windows that weren't easy to open or close, and floorboards so rotten I sometimes imagined I was going to drop straight through to the floor below. That apartment was impressive in its dilapidated way, definitely a couple of steps above the places where most of us were living. And it was a great location. "Burt," I remember her yelling as she came through the door one afternoon, "put on your shoes, just around the corner there's a terrific chair sitting on the street. Somebody must've left it out with the trash. Fast. Before it's gone." Some of the same stuff that was in that apartment, Marcia's old stuff, is around me now: the Art Nouveau lamps (Marcia boasted about buying them for a couple of dollars at the Salvation Army) and even the Victorian sofa with its curving back, another piece she had me drag off the street—and then dragged with her all the way to New York and then back to what I guess will be its final resting place here in Marin.

But I was going to say something about that party—the last one she threw while I was living with her. Started out simple that night. Five bottles of wine lined up on the table in the dining room. The first people to arrive were three or four guys from the *Chronicle*. They brought a couple more bottles, French. I was shy around them, not even sure they knew I was Marcia's boyfriend. Marcia wasn't big on explanations. "Keep 'em guessing," she liked to say. Then Jack, Mike, Jack's wife, and Mike's girl arrived, along with other people from Berkeley days, some of whom I never really knew, at best knew only slightly. The drinks table was starting to get messy. One bottle two-thirds full. Another almost empty. Another half full. Somebody appeared with a bottle of Pernod. "Do you have any club soda?" I was trying to keep it simple.

There's a folder labeled "Parties" in one of Marcia's drawers, but there isn't much in it, only a couple of pages. "How do you write about parties? Begin with groups? Individuals? Look at parties in Proust. Aren't there some great Greenwich Village parties in *The Recognitions*? See how Gaddis did it. Begin with what I remember best. The couple of times when the old upright piano in the living room got a workout. Set the scene. You came into the living room, biggest of the four rooms. In between that and the kitchen was the room where I wrote or tried to write. I guess it was supposed to be the dining room. Beyond the kitchen were the bathroom and the bedroom. It was a big kitchen with a long marble counter along one wall. A great apartment, but a strange apartment. No hallway. You got to one room through the other. The old upright piano. I'd grown up with it. Mom let me take it with me. The evening Bev Kelly appeared, the jazz singer. I didn't know her." I'm going to fill in a little here. Somebody brought Bev Kelly late, it must have been after her set at The Coffee Gallery, I think that's where she was performing. It was a year or two later that her first album came out. I think it was called *Beverly Kelly Sings*. I was in the kitchen. People were standing packed tight. (Why is the kitchen where people always congregate?) I was talking to some bore from the *Chronicle*. I didn't want to offend him—he was one of Marcia's colleagues. I tried to keep up with whatever the hell he was saying about Bay Area politics. Then Mike was at my elbow. "Burt, you've got a star in the living room, Jack's trying to get her to sing." The *Chronicle* guy turned to Mike. "Who?" "Bev Kelly." "I saw her the other night. Fantastic."

Back to Marcia's manuscript. "Everybody piled into the living room. Across the room, Jack and two other guys were hovering over a small woman, small head, short blond hair, sitting on the ottoman, cigarette in one hand, the hand under her chin, drink in the other hand, self-contained, resisting Jack's importuning. Jack, forever loyal to Evelyn, was a big charmer when it came to conversations at dinners and parties. 'One song, Miss Kelly. Sing "My Ship."' She did. I just found 'My Ship' on an LP of Kelly's, *Love Locked Out*, that I seem to have held onto all these years. I wiped the dust off the old vinyl. Now I've listened to it again. Ira Gershwin lyrics; Kurt Weill music. Some guy who must've come with her sat down at the piano. She stood next to him. A subdued voice. Dulled grandeur—tarnished gold—as she sang about the ship with sails of silk and decks trimmed with gold. 'I can wait the years / Till it appears.' The voice was low, some might say depressed, an old-fashioned nightclub chanteuse reimagining herself in the midst of the take-it-or-leave-it mood of the 1950s. She was the bummed-out tragedian. People crowded around the rather elegant old upright piano; sitting on top of it was a vase holding some dried branches with red berries. Bev Kelly was abstracted, not really looking at anybody. Not acting. Corny phrase—the singing came from the heart—but true. What a depressed song, all about the ship that never comes, the love that never comes. And yet we loved it. There was applause, but only after an awed delay. I wonder if anybody would dare stand up and sing something at a party now."

That's where Marcia's writing trails off. Maybe she was feeling uneasy about the rest of the evening, because it was the beginning of the end of our first time around (or our second time if you count our brief college fling). The night Bev Kelly sang, although it was already late, her performance gave the party a shot in the arm. I heard somebody on the phone, "Do you know what just happened over here?" New people started to arrive—people I didn't know. Bev Kelly didn't sing anything else and left soon after, but Marcia's was the place to be. Somebody went out for more wine and beer. Marcia had disappeared. She liked to duck out of her own parties for a quarter of an hour, go down into the alley and have a cigarette and a confidential conversation with I don't know who. She liked the idea that things went on without her. I think it gave her a sense of power. She was the invisible hand, the impresario behind the curtain. I didn't think anything much when I didn't see her for an hour or so, not even when it was just me and Ginny and a couple of other friends staying to give a hand, bringing the empties into the kitchen, washing up. Marcia reappeared just as we were finishing. She'd gone out for a drink with Kelly and the pianist. She said he was Kelly's boyfriend, though not for much longer. How she knew that—or at least thought it—I have no idea.

For all I know she didn't know what she was talking about when it came to Bev Kelly and her boyfriend. It occurs to me that she might have been thinking about her own boyfriend, me at the time. She may have suspected that we weren't going to be together much longer. I know I've already sort of blamed her for our breakup. I guess that's what I was implying when I said she was restless, unwilling to devote a lot of time and energy to somebody she'd already fooled around with some in college. But enough of trying to figure out Marcia's side of the story. I guess I'm under some obligation to tell my side. I get along with women. Always have. I was popular with the girls in high school and college. And after Marcia more or less threw me out of her apartment I had no trouble finding somebody else who was happy to shack up with me. Several women, as a matter of fact. I've been told I'm adorable. I can also be unreliable. Otherwise I guess I would've been married long ago. Maybe also divorced. Marcia was exciting to be with. And she was sweet about me. She said I was charming. She said I was great in bed. But when I was feeling diffident or maybe laconic she accused me of being a depressive. I'm not sure she was right. But whether she was right or wrong there were definitely things about me she didn't like. With Marcia it was always a bit of a roller coaster.

When Marcia came back to San Francisco and we started up again—that was in 1965—I figured it would end in a matter of months. Maybe that's what she expected. But one morning, a couple of weeks after we'd gotten back together, she looked at me across the table and said, "You know Burt, maybe you're a keeper." I was taken aback. So I responded with a joke. "I'll be kept." But I meant it. Later that day, since neither of us felt like doing anything constructive, we went into the city, to the Palace of the Legion of Honor with its gorgeous views of the bay. Marcia was eager to see a show of paintings by Renoir. I vaguely remembered a big Renoir show there back in the 1940s and now, twenty years later, they were doing Renoir again. I was surprised that Marcia was interested. Wasn't Renoir for middlebrows? I suspected that she wanted to go so she could declare the show a midcult disaster. Among the few critics she approved of was Dwight Macdonald, and especially his long essay "Masscult and Midcult," which had appeared a few years earlier. She loved something she'd once heard him say at a party in New York, that only when he offered a negative judgment could he be sure he was right. But from the moment we walked into the Renoir show Marcia was very quiet. She stopped for the longest time in front of *The Luncheon of the Boating Party*, the big canvas with a group of bohemian friends enjoying a casual lunch on a sunny day, We talked about the wonderful informality of the painting—the crisscrossing flirtations, the fellow sitting backward on a chair. Finally Marcia announced, pointing to the pretty young woman kissing the little dog, "That's pleasure, that's love, that's perfection." It was then that I realized there was something of a Renoir woman in Marcia's softly rounded features and blurred blue eyes.

5: NICK

In *A Night at the Opera* I didn't just profile the big names—Pierre Boulez and Italo Calvino and the rest of the stars of that crazy Roman production—but also an usher, a propman. People liked that. Maybe I'll do the same here. Maybe write a few pages about Nick, the quietest of madmen, skeletal, with a scruffy beard. I've heard women say they find him handsome. I can't see it. As it happens, although I don't get to bookstores much anymore, I gather, incredibly enough, Nick is still working at the bookstore after all these years. City Lights. That crazy corner location in North Beach (the same building was for a time the home of A. Cavalli & Company, an Italian bookstore). I'll keep my remarks to what I remember, City Lights back then. Upstairs, the place was tiny, shaped to fit into the wedge where two streets meet. People stood around reading the magazines until they were too dog-eared for anybody to ever buy them. I never had the impression that they sold much of anything, aside from copies of Allen's *Kaddish*. (Do I really need to say which Allen?)

Downstairs was the bigger space, where Nick presided over the paperbacks. It was all or at least mostly all paperbacks, that was the point, hardbacks were for your parents. Managers came and went, but Nick went on and on, the beard still wispy, the kind an adolescent tries to grow. He knew everything about those damn paperbacks. It wasn't a knowledge of books, exactly, but of editions, introductions, translations, what was in print and going out of print and coming back. He became emotional when he discussed the closing of a paperback line. "It's that executive they hired from the ad agency," he growled, his eyes narrowing, convinced there was some kind of conspiracy. Nick squirreled stuff away in a back room, five copies of what he said was the better translation of this or that. He would sneak a book out for a special friend even though this particular edition wasn't supposed to be in circulation, certainly not to be sold in a bookstore, on account of some copyright dispute. He knew about such things. Larry Ferlinghetti, who founded the place with Peter (Peter Martin, who was a college professor and the son of the Italian anarchist Carlo Tresca), wasn't a details guy. Nick, although too much the dreamer to ever manage the place, or so people assumed, was definitely the man with the details. He kept the City Lights engine running.

Nick's career, such as it was or maybe still is, would have been unimaginable without the paperback revolution. I'm not sure he saw the pomposity in his populism, the absurd pride he took in the H. P. Lovecraft stories in scuzzy paperbacks with lurid covers that he'd bought from a failing Brooklyn publisher. "Got everything they had in the warehouse before it was pulped," he proudly announced.

I don't give a damn about Lovecraft, but I do give Nick credit for recognizing that the bookstore couldn't necessarily survive on books about Zen and the Beats. He had customers in the movie industry who came up from LA every couple of months just to see what lurid B novels he'd found, strange sci-fi stories, the covers featuring women with breasts practically bursting out of their minimalist space suits. He presented those idiotic volumes with a seriousness that would have seemed comic if it weren't for Nick's immunity to irony. He was hardly the only friend—I guess I can call him a friend—who failed to see the comedy in our avant-garde attitudes. What was that about? Was everybody afraid that if they made light of their own wayward ways they risked losing the battle with corporate America? (As if corporate America cared.) Nick was incapable of laughing at himself. Frankly, he was a sort of snob—he treated obscure paperbacks as if they were rare editions. But Nick's pretensions made those Hollywood producers feel good. They were impressed by his bohemian seriousness—at least up to a point. For a while there was talk that one of the books that had come out of the basement of City Lights was going to become a major movie. It died somewhere in development—like every other Hollywood deal our crowd dreamed up.

Was Nick happy? Was Nick sad? He seemed even-tempered, aside from those muffled outbursts about publishers whom he must have understood were just trying to keep their heads above water. Nick sometimes mistook those publishers for moguls when the truth was that most of them were operating on the slimmest profit margins when they were seeing any profit at all. Mostly Nick struck me as contained—emotionally, but physically, too. He didn't seem to take up any space. Customers slid by him without noticing. I don't understand people who can disappear like that. Nothing could be stranger to somebody like me, incapable as I am of keeping anything in. I'm loudmouthed, overbearing—so they say. When you asked Nick why or how he never lost his cool—and customers could sure be a pain in the ass—he put it down to Buddhism, his bookish Buddhism, picked up from paperbacks and small press publications, koans, haikus, prayers, and sermons, all translated into English. His Buddhism had been fueled by the poet Dave Jones. Jones was no friend of mine and too grand and reclusive to tolerate San Francisco for long, but on his infrequent appearances in town, down for a day from some Napa or Sonoma retreat, he liked to end up at City Lights, the grizzled poet talking with Nick about his time in Japan.

Nick revered poets—all poets—and for him Dave was the poet's poet. "The wild crazy austerity of Dave Jones's poetry," I once heard him murmur, apropos of nothing and so far as I could see without meaning to address anybody in particular. He certainly couldn't get enough of Dave's picaresque accounts of his adventures in the Orient. Dave told Nick about the half-collapsed rooms in Japanese monasteries (they could be rented for next to nothing); the maple trees with their autumn oranges and purples that looked hallucinogenic (even if you weren't already high); the pale moon in the palest early morning sky; the rocky beaches with the salt water seeping into your skin; the chants and the bells and the crazy hats that some of the monks wore; and the furtive nights away from the holy place looking for some exotic cunt. Dave pronounced *cunt* carefully, for impact, and maybe Nick was a little shocked, but he disguised that as best he could, swallowing hard, his Adam's apple more prominent than ever.

Dave gave Nick his Japanese fever, and Nick fed it with the Asian books in the religion and poetry sections downstairs at City Lights. Then a Japanese girl appeared in the basement, looking for a copy of one of D. H. Lawrence's novels, a student at San Francisco State, bespectacled, long black hair. Next thing we knew, she was crazy about Nick. Nick didn't really know all that much about Japan, aside from Dave's tall tales. As for the girl, she was hearing about a Japan that she'd never even imagined, despite having grown up over there. Her forward-looking family had no interest in moss-covered outhouses in godforsaken monasteries. Then she graduated and was going back and Nick, who for all anybody knew lived downstairs in the bowels of City Lights, packed his knapsack and turned his savings into traveler's checks and was going to Japan with her. Is anybody surprised that it didn't work out? At first postcards arrived. Nick and the girl—her name was Mary—were traveling around the country, seeing some of the sights Dave had told Nick about. The postcards were the Buddhist backpacker's version of "Having a great time. Wish you were here." I still have one of them. The picture, in lurid colors, is of some rock garden, though not the one everybody knows. And on the back is this:

> "Sun on old stones
> I explode in laughter."
> —Love to you Marcia, from Bashō/Nick.

I knew a bit about Bashō, a seventeenth-century Zen Buddhist poet, but suspected that Nick had made up the poem. I was surprised Nick thought to send me a card.

It seemed they were having a good time. But it didn't last. Mary's parents had met Nick but not exactly understood that Mary was going off with him. When they reappeared in Tokyo and it began to dawn on Mom and Dad that Mary was serious about the weird American, they read her the riot act and she bowed to their wishes. Her San Francisco adventure was over. Nick decided to return to some monastery on one of the less traveled islands. Don't ask me the name. There he settled down in one of those falling-apart old monk's cells that Dave had described with such panache. What happened after that nobody ever really knew, except that Dave sent Nick a ticket back to SF and he returned to the basement at City Lights and that was that. There were rumors about his having some trouble with a village girl and leaving town in a hurry, before the villagers had a chance to boil him in oil. I find it hard to imagine, but maybe it was what he thought Dave would've done. Maybe so, but of course Dave would never have been caught. I think I saw Nick in the store only once after he returned. I asked him, "So how was Japan?" I should have kept my mouth shut. "Oh, Marcia," he came back, "you couldn't understand what it meant to me. To you it's all kitsch and gore, *Madame Butterfly* and Mishima novels."

6: PARENTS

Marcia always said she loved Cocteau's *Les Parents terribles*. Whatever she actually thought about the movie and Jean Marais's over-the-top performance as an overaged adolescent, I think what she liked most of all was the sheer impudence of the title. She never said much about her parents, even when we were all hanging out together in our twenties and people liked to complain about Mom and Dad. I never said much about mine either, but they were a couple of hours away in Carmel while hers were living in the same city as us, breathing down her neck. Maybe a certain immunity to the power of the parental unit was part of what we had in common. As her boyfriend for a time, I did end up meeting them. That there's hardly a word about them anywhere in the stuff she wrote doesn't surprise me. They weren't terrible parents. Anything but. I think she found them absurd, or found it absurd that she was their daughter, their beloved and adored daughter, their only child, whom they supported, I mean materially, though how much I didn't realize until recently. She was secretive about money. I'm not sure I would include Mr. and Mrs.

Lang here, except that they come up—or at least their money comes up—in some of Marcia's letters to Mike a few years later. But there's something more. They were Europeans, products of Berlin in the 1920s. The more I think about it the more I wonder if Marcia didn't inherit a wild streak from some secret past of theirs.

When it came to dealing with the Langs—and she did deal with them, without really talking much about it—Marcia discovered that my ambition to own and operate a little printing press was a plus. She pretended to be amused that her father, who owned Lang Fine Wines and Spirits, said to be San Francisco's most prestigious liquor store, thought I might turn out to be a fellow entrepreneur, running a successful business. Actually I think her feelings were somewhere between bemused and annoyed. Mr. Lang had never quite gotten over her refusal to marry a guy headed to law school whom she'd dated for a time at Berkeley. She told me after I first met her parents that her father said I was an improvement over the last one. If I ever knew who that was I can't remember now. Somehow Mr. Lang had decided that my interest in the press might lead to a more stable kind of profession, slipping their errant daughter into something like respectability. It wasn't that the Langs didn't know what their daughter was up to. They were proud that she wanted to be a writer. Writing was fine. But Marcia needed to get married. There had to be a breadwinner in the family. And she needed to have children. I think they were a little confused by me, maybe because I wasn't Jewish. They couldn't quite figure me out. When I put on a jacket and a tie and slicked back and combed my hair I could pass for an all-American guy with a future in the business world. The Langs could at least hope that I wasn't another one of their daughter's loser bohemian boyfriends.

Mr. and Mrs. Lang kept the past past. They didn't talk about where they'd come from or what they'd gone through. I'm not sure I would have ever realized that Marcia had not only been born in Berlin but had lived there into early adolescence if I hadn't pressed her about a few fairly offbeat pieces of German modernist silver that her parents had in the breakfront in the dining room. There were also, hanging in the living room, a couple of angular landscapes by a German Expressionist whose name I can't remember. I *should* know that name, since those canvases are now hanging right here in this room in Marin. My drawing a blank may have something to do with Marcia's having been so damn evasive about growing up in Germany, and when the family left there, and the couple of years they spent in England before they made it to the USA. Apparently back in their Berlin days her parents had been susceptible to the avant-garde, at least that's what the modernist silver and the Expressionist paintings suggest. But my sense is that they left all that behind when they got out of Germany—which was early, a couple of years before Kristallnacht, Mr. Lang was always thinking ahead. Did it bother Mom and Pop that I wasn't Jewish? Yes and no. They weren't religious. Back in Berlin I doubt they'd walked into a synagogue more than once or twice a year. But after the Holocaust? Marcia told me her mother had said, "The children will be Jewish, whether he converts or not." They belonged to a big synagogue in San Francisco but I think that was mostly because Mr. Lang needed the connections for business. A Jewish liquor store needed a Jewish clientele.

Going to dinner in their house on a street over by the Pacific was strange. You wouldn't have necessarily known from the way they lived that Marcia's father had become a fairly wealthy man. Everything that wasn't absolutely essential was being saved for a rainy day. You couldn't blame people who had gotten out of Germany at the right moment for worrying about rainy days. Their house was like a padded cell, designed to protect against the world's dirt, chaos, and bad vibes. The wall-to-wall carpeting was so thick that you couldn't hear your footsteps. The bathroom was so terrifyingly clean that I was almost afraid to take a leak. Under the thick damask tablecloth on the dining table there were pads that protected the wooden surface. I never actually saw the bare table, but Marcia told me about it, though she herself had hardly ever seen it. For normal meals in the dining room they ate on the pads without even covering them with a tablecloth. The house was suffocating, but so different from the way that Marcia and I and our friends were living at the time that it had a weird fascination, at least for me. Marcia tried to maintain a stony silence during our visits. Her answers to questions—about her job at the *Chronicle*, about what she was writing—were monosyllabic. Her parents, who seemed to regard their only child in some kind of messianic light, were afraid to push further. I think her mother secretly enjoyed her daughter's rebellious streak. As for me, as I said, her father was desperate to imagine that my miniscule printing enterprise was the beginning of something more. When I explained that my grandfather had given me the couple of hundred dollars to get started, he nodded approvingly, as if he were witnessing the beginning of an entrepreneurial empire. Little did he know.

A few weeks ago, running into Mike at the Silver Spur, I mentioned that Marcia never talked about her parents. He said that he had worked for Mr. Lang for a time, something I must have known but for some reason forgot. During his last year at Berkeley Mike took a job at Lang Fine Wines and Spirits for a few of the busy weeks around Christmas. Mr. Lang was so impressed that he offered Mike a job when he graduated—hoping, I suppose, to set another one of Marcia's vagrant friends on the straight and narrow. Mike worked there for a year before he found a job teaching English in one of the private schools. He said that after watching Marcia's father in action, he'd concluded that her taste for intrigue and playing both sides came from Mr. Lang. Mike saw him with the suppliers—pushing for better prices, insisting on certain vintages, suggesting that if the competition was stocking that thirty-year-old bourbon he wouldn't touch it. He was tough. Then there was Mr. Lang with the better customers, all silky and charming, a well-tailored jacket slipped over the shirtsleeves that were good enough for the suppliers, suddenly careful to make sure that his watch, one that the San Francisco matrons would respect, was low on his wrist, visible beneath the jacket cuff. Mike's specialty was organizing the little surprise gifts that the best customers received gratis, not just for Christmas but for birthdays and, if the family was Jewish, in the run-up to the High Holy Days. Lang Fine Wines and Spirits was a fancy outfit.

Mr. and Mrs. Lang were a pleasant looking couple, an attractive couple, which to my young eyes meant there was nothing that stood out. Mr. Lang was middle height, no excess weight, his face nicely lined. I suppose Mrs. Lang would be described as birdlike, relatively short skirts, good ankles, full-breasted, her wide face framed by hair cut surprisingly short for a middle-aged matron. The hair was swept up from her brow, a boyish style maybe left over from her fun-loving younger days in Berlin. Marcia had inherited her lovely blue eyes.

7: CALIFORNIA SCHOOL OF FINE ARTS

Spanish style. It's everywhere you turn in California, the stucco walls, arches, colonnades, patterned tiles on apartment buildings, post offices, schools, as if everything were the set for some deadly dull Holly-wood movie. I hated it from the minute I arrived on the West Coast as a teenager. Still do. The Bay Area may not be as bad as Los Angeles, but even in Northern California the Spanish stuff can drive me crazy, the way corners are softened into a curve, beige on beige buildings, cacti, and the flowering bougainvillea, a travel poster advertising a slightly exotic version of home sweet home. The best you can do is try and ignore it. That's what we did at the California School of Fine Arts. Somebody called it a "quintessential" Spanish-style masterpiece of the 1930s. I worked in a cramped little office for close to four years when I was just out of Berkeley. What did I do? I filled out half-finished forms for the guys studying painting on the GI bill and cleaned up whatever administrative mess had been left by Douglas MacAgy, the director, a visionary who was buddies with some of the Abstract Expressionists but was incapable of following through on an invoice, a payroll, much less a budget. I was the office manager, something like that. I got the job at a party. Everything happened at parties. Jermayne, MacAgy's wife at the time, a curator known for wonderfully crazy shows including one on trompe l'oeil painting as more or less proto-Surrealism, was complaining that his assistant, who wasn't much good anyway, had left and he was going out of his mind. I told her I was looking for a job. She pulled him over and he said I should come by the next morning. He hired me on the spot. I'd been surviving on crappy part-time jobs since graduating from college a year earlier and was up for just about anything. A full-time job in an art school—it sounded like heaven.

Art schools are locker rooms for guys who were never any good at sports. There's male bonding, male competition, the same heat and stress—and the barely dressed models might as well be cheerleaders. There was definitely a smell of sex around the school, something in the air thick with turpentine and oil paint, the models in thin robes walking around the studio during breaks, checking out the guys and the work the guys were doing—of course it was mostly guys. A couple of the advanced instructors would have nothing to do with the models; they were totally into abstract art and worried that drawing or painting from life was a reactionary gesture. But back then that remained a minority view. Most of the instructors still believed that drawing from a model was the way to learn the basics. You didn't need anybody to remind you that Cubism had been invented by artists who knew how to draw the figure. Anyway, in addition to whatever models there were in the classes—and there were still plenty—the students organized their own informal after-hours sessions, sometimes hiring girls or guys but sometimes with the students taking turns on the modeling stand. It was interesting to see who would take off what. A couple of the girls just walked right up there and stripped. So did a couple of the guys. Others kept on a bra and panties or a pair of underpants. Jack Johanson modeled completely dressed. Arrogant guy. Figured he was an eyeful no matter what. The once or twice I modeled I took it all off, no compunctions. But when MacAgy heard about my performance he was pissed. That was the end of my modeling career. Who wants to hold still for thirty minutes, anyway?

Everybody took themselves so damn seriously. That was the lunacy and the wonder of the school. When an artist with a New York reputation appeared to teach for a few months—there was Mark Rothko for a time and for a longer time Clyfford Still—the boys followed the big guy's every move, adopting his brand of cigarettes, eager to know what kind of whiskey he drank. Then there was Jean Zinser, who although he was always around and didn't have the New York cachet, somehow managed to hold the attention of more students than even the big names from elsewhere. He worked at it. Zinser was a master seducer, with his sleepy eyes and Cheshire grin. The guys were a long way from home and he was always around. He was a prophet, a good listener, a shrink, a mindfuck—the wayward dad they never had. "The labyrinth!" he would announce the first day of the semester. "If you don't enter you'll never become an artist. You must be both Theseus and the Minotaur!" I don't know why the students didn't laugh in his face. Some of them had been in combat and seen real blood and gore. What did they want with this phony-baloney labyrinth? Easy enough to wonder now. Back then the labyrinth seemed new, or new-old. "Make the labyrinth real!" Zinser intoned. A week or two into the fall semester, strange structures began to appear in the big courtyard with the Spanish-style colonnades. Driftwood, rusty iron, tin cans, anything would do. The students, most of them well into their twenties, looked ridiculous out there, soldiers reduced to building deranged dollhouses. An older instructor muttered, "Zinser's turning soldiers into sissy boys."

Where Mr. Z came from, nobody seemed to know. He had a plummy accent, the sort of thing you'd pick up in a drama class, not the capitals of Europe. I'm not sure he'd ever been to Europe. He sometimes announced, "I'm a real American, with a Mexican mother and a Canadian father." It was hard to imagine that this strange man, a prophet with his homespun philosophy, had ever been a child. I'd sat at the back of his class now and then as he revved up the students. "The labyrinth is a rite," he'd declare. "Of course there's the labyrinth of Greek mythology, but every civilization has its labyrinth, just ask the archaeologists who study Pre-Columbian cultures." Zinser wanted his students to be avid—for everything. "You see," he would insist, "you can't just talk to other artists—you have to talk to everybody. I've learned more about art from archaeologists and anthropologists than from most of the artists I know."

Jack Johanson was the monitor in Zinser's painting class. I'd see him and Mr. Z before or after class, by the door of the studio. Zinser, not fat but definitely soft around the edges, was almost always wearing a pair of faded blue-jean overalls; he looked like an old-time union organizer. Jack was lean and concise, always with his sweatshirt and cowboy boots. For eight or so months, Jack and Zinser were locked in a student-mentor embrace. I don't mean sexual. This was strictly platonic. Zinser had a wife at home and Jack was already seeing Evelyn. I'd get reports on their conversations from Jack; he'd pull me out of my office for a cigarette. "Zinser was on a roll today." Jack was on a bench behind my office, half reclining, smoking, the smoke curling up past his moustache, waved away from his eyes with his free hand. He was telling me that Zinser had been yelling at the class. "You're all lost in the labyrinth," Jack quoted. Having sent the students into the labyrinth, Zinser was now excoriating them for not knowing how or when to get out. "You've gotta fuck with their minds," he'd told Jack, but in confidence.

It was funny to hear Jack imitate Zinser. He wasn't very good at it. "You've gotta find your way out. How do you do that?" Then Jack described Mr. Z turning on shy, arrogant Evelyn. There were only two girls in the class; she was the looker. "What would a woman know about the labyrinth?" So Mr. Z began. "It's a man's work, getting out. You, my dear, are Penelope, weaving and unweaving, waiting for—" and, yes, then Mr. Z looked at Jack. Jack seemed to think Zinser was damn clever, turning Evelyn into Penelope, or maybe what he liked was that this made him Odysseus. As for Evelyn's feelings, when I asked Jack about that he said he hadn't noticed. "Anyway," he added, "Evelyn takes everything in stride." Jack was busy attending to Mr. Z's needs, running the projector as he lectured to the students. Jack recounted his comments as if they were gospel. "Okay everybody, brushes down," Mr. Z would begin. "We're going to look at some things. You better start thinking—thinking hard, thinking ideas—or you're never really going to be a painter. You're all too hung up on the Surrealists. Or that Gorky you saw in last month's *Art News*. You've gotta discover something for yourself." Mr. Z had shown, so Jack told me, watery cataclysms drawn by Leonardo da Vinci, the intricate arabesques of Persian carpets, photographs of Indian astronomical observatories with weird staircases leading nowhere, and slides of physics experiments with sprays of tiny white dots. By the end of class Mr. Z was shouting: "This is the new labyrinth!" Jack thought it was pretty cool.

Jack could seem imperturbable, docile, in those early months, at Mr. Z's beck and call, dealing efficiently with broken projectors, missing easels, and window shades that failed to go up or down. But at other times Mr. Z's favorite student, who was turning twenty-five, couldn't help wondering if there was any future in labyrinths, at least the kind that Zinser had been painting for a decade and exhibiting in San Francisco and, once or twice, in New York. "I'm not showing it to Mr. Z," Jack said as he handed me a little notebook, three by five inches, full of drawings of Evelyn in his apartment, reading a book, listening to music, bare-breasted in bed, her long limbs outlined in India ink. "It's my Penelope notebook," he said, only half ironically. There was an air of apostasy about Jack's little notebook. "Maybe this is the real labyrinth," Jack said, aware I might find the comment corny. "No. Really, Marcia. I'm serious. Joyce turned Greece into Dublin. Why not SF? You know I've been looking at Greek vase painting. Those really simple lines."

When did Zinser realize that Jack was breaking ranks? In those overalls of his, Mr. Z could look like an idiot, or maybe an idiot savant. But it took close calculation to hold on to as many of the smartest students as he did, year after year. By the time Jack was in his second year with Zinser it must have been clear to Mr. Z that something was up. They talked about the big abstraction that Jack had been working on in class, jagged forms in excitable colors. But a student who'd been to Jack's apartment told Mr. Z that at home he was working on a painting of Evelyn in bed, buck naked in a tangle of sheets. Come the final spring show of student work, there she was—Jack's portrait of Evelyn hanging in the middle of the big room. "He told me I've lost my nerve." Jack came into my office to tell me this. "The nerve of *him*." But somebody heard Zinser muttering, as he left the opening, "That Jack, smart boy. He's made Evelyn the new idol." From what Jack has told me, Zinser never spoke to him again, even after Jack returned to the school as an adjunct instructor.

8: THE SAN FRANCISCO PUPPET TROUPE

The biggest nightmare of my San Francisco days was working with a couple, Jane and Jonas O'Doherty, on the San Francisco Puppet Troupe. I'm reminded of that hell by some lines in Wyndham Lewis's autobiographical book, *Rude Assignment.* (Great title.) "Avant-gardism in itself, at any time, is not a merit or a demerit. Some people are the changers and some the conservers." The more successful that damn puppet theater got, the clearer it became that Jane wanted to be a changer and Jonas wanted to be conserver and never the twain would meet. Jane, who'd grown up on a farm, hadn't finished college and had a chip on her shoulder. She was desperate to earn as many merit points as she could as an experimentalist, an original. Jonas, who had gone to Stanford, was beginning to think that demerits were the way to go. His mother was a famous bohemian (rumored affairs with Hemingway and various lesser lights), so maybe he was trying to set himself apart from her, I'm not sure. I'm not much for giving advice, but if I have one piece to hand down, it's never work with a couple on some kind of mom-and-pop operation. When they don't get along they'll turn against you to prove that they're actually united about something. They'll chew you up when they aren't chewing each other up. If it hadn't been for Jane and Jonas maybe I would've never left San Francisco. I guess I have them to thank for my so-called career.

I got to know Jonas my first year working at the school. Late on Wednesday afternoons, when the regular classes were over, he ran a workshop on marionette making. He wasn't really on staff. MacAgy, who liked to talk about the Ballets Russes and the Bauhaus and wanted to resurrect that old modern merger of the visual and theatrical arts, the Gesamtkunstwerk, gave Jonas a check for ten dollars for each session. (I know. I wrote the checks.) Eight or ten students generally appeared. Jonas, who was in his early thirties, blended right in. He was a few years older than some of the students but still looked like a kid, with his big open face and red hair cut short in what I've always thought of as a hipster crew cut; later, in New York, I realized it was John Cage's look. Jonas worked his ass off for that class. He'd arrive a couple of hours before the workshop began and slowly, methodically unpack the hardware store's worth of stuff he kept in a couple of old trunks in the back corner of one of the drawing studios. When the students wandered in later in the afternoon and gathered around him the scene suggested the sorcerer and his apprentices. Jonas was in his element.

If I was blindsided a few years later by the screaming arguments between husband and wife about what a puppet theater ought to be, I guess it was because Jonas had been so damn quiet and concentrated in those workshops. Nothing even remotely theoretical ever came up. Everything was about how to make a puppet move in a particular way. Jonas might start the students off by attaching a hand to an arm with a tiny hook and eye. Within a month he was engaged in intense one-on-one conversations, recommending a ball bearing as the best way to attach a head to a neck. "It's elementary physics," I'd hear Jonas patiently explain to a young painter who'd nearly flunked out of a college engineering course and was relieved to be in an art school. What the marionettes were made of or actually looked like—folkloric carved wood, futuristic metal, funky papier-mâché—didn't seem to matter all that much to Jonas. Later I realized that he did have strong opinions. Violent opinions, in fact. But he was uncertain as to where he stood at the school. So he kept his mouth shut when it came to Futurism versus Expressionism. "It's all pulleys and levers, pulleys and levers," he would say to a bewildered aesthete who an hour earlier had been happily dripping paint à la Pollock.

On afternoons when Jonas appeared, I'd watch the goings on from the back of the studio. If the students were keeping busy Jonas would come over and talk. When I was in college I'd worked backstage at the theater club for a couple of months. I liked the nitty-gritty of theater. Years later I would be in my element in Rome, hanging out with the stagehands at the Opera House, watching a multimedia spectacle called *And Then There Were None*... come into being—and then writing about everything I'd seen. I've always been somewhere between an addict and a skeptic when it comes to the theater. I love the illusions although as often as not I don't think they really work. So I liked Jonas's levelheaded approach, the way he talked about the old Punch and Judy puppet theater. That was his greatest passion.

When I went to one of the performances that he and Jane were putting on, my feeling was that they had gotten it just right. They rented, maybe they were just given, a room at the back of The Coffee Gallery for a night. It was a kind of storeroom, hot as hell with a couple dozen people crowded in. I was impressed by the fresh spin they brought to the old routines, a mix of Punch and Judy and Pierrot and Pierrette, with the wisecracking marionettes spouting Preston Sturges style dialogue, jokes about the latest consumer products, accompanied by some bebop jazz. The sets were sweetly garish Victoriana, deep blue and red, lemon yellow and purple, with nifty crosshatching in black and white to suggest old-fashioned engravings. I laughed. I was impressed. I kept up with their shows. But it was only a few years later, when I had become totally fed up with my job at the *Chronicle*, that I had what I thought was a brilliant idea. Jonas and Jane were always running out of money. They weren't getting much of anything for the few performances they managed to do. What if I became their manager and made them the toast of San Francisco?

They came over to my place for dinner, Jonas with his crew cut and Jane with her long dark hair and Nefertiti eyes. We hit it off, at least I thought we did. I talked and they listened, that may have been what threw me off. In retrospect, I imagine Jane lying in wait, planning to use me and abuse me. But that's probably unfair. She lived in the moment. For the moment I was what she needed. A few years before, I'd seen MacAgy working moneyed San Francisco on behalf of the school, and I figured I could find a little bit of Nob Hill dough to fund some puppet theater performances in schools, hospitals, old age homes, and parks. Maybe I'd find enough so that Jane could give up her job sewing blouses for a fancy dress shop and Jonas wouldn't have to do electrical jobs for a design firm. Maybe I could quit the *Chronicle*. Within weeks I had old Gladys Fleischman and the Fleischman Foundation lined up. Jane and Jonas thought I was a genius. We got a series of gigs in hospitals, old age homes, and elementary schools. We had a great run that spring. Then summer came and all hell broke loose. It turned out that Jane hated Punch and Judy and the clever costumes she turned out on her sewing machine. Now that we were cooking—that's how she put it—she wanted to do Pirandello and Kafka, with cinematic effects. "Let's break the mold. Take it further. I'm sick of sequins and harlequin diamonds." The fights would start mildly, with Jonas cajoling, "Jane, please, we do this so well." But she took a harder and harder line: "I'm not going to stand there again, on my feet for an hour, doing Pierrot and Pierrette. Who gives a shit?"

What I'd missed was that Jane had an agenda—Leftist, Existentialist. She had a point she wanted to make. What I'd taken as loving renditions of the old marionette theater—French, Italian, Sicilian, I was vague on the particulars—were actually souped up, at least so Jane believed, with some Marxist or maybe it was Trotskyite additions. Let's not forget that those were the years when Republicans in Washington were looking for Commies under every bed. I will say this for Jane—she was a little ahead of the curve in her fearless antiestablishment views. In Jane's mind the doctor, lawyer, and shopkeeper marionettes that crossed paths with Punch and Judy were archetypes of oppression, not exactly the clever riffs on classical types that most of the audience probably imagined they were. At first Jane's radicalism was pretty much subtext. And to the extent that her intentions were clear, that was a plus with some of Jane's Lefty friends, who made up a not insignificant part of their very small audience. But the more the audience grew and the more amused people were, the more Jane wanted to disabuse them. People were perfectly content with some light mockery of what Jane referred to as "the power structure." After all, this was San Francisco, with its Wobblies and longshoremen. Even the San Francisco gentry weren't opposed to controversy, at least up to a point. But just as we were getting a bit better known around town, Jane, who mistook an attentive audience for an audience that was on her wavelength, decided to sew a sequined swastika onto the shopkeeper's costume and give Punch a hammer and sickle in place of his good old-fashioned baton. I found myself forced to explain what we were doing to the vice-principal of an elementary school and the assistant director of a nursing home. They were sympathetic. They were on our side. But couldn't we tone it down?

I decided to test the waters late one night, when I'd taken Jane and Jonas back to my place for pasta after a performance that had gone pretty well. I began to make my pitch as I stood waiting for a large pot of water to boil and Jane and Jonas sat next to each other, each with a glass of wine, at the old round oak table. "You know the swastika and the hammer and sickle are making some people uncomfortable," I said. I can't say that I was surprised when Jane immediately responded, "I don't give a fuck. Let's up the ante." I turned from the stove to look at them, thinking maybe I should have waited until we were eating—or done eating. Jonas was looking down into his wineglass. Then his head popped up—abruptly, jerkily, like (sorry) a marionette. He was looking at her, looking hard. And he said, in a voice that he obviously meant to be amused or laid-back but was really anything but, "Fuck you." He immediately regretted it. He could see that she didn't think it was funny. "I'm sorry, I'm just kidding." "Sure you're kidding—you're kidding yourself," was her response. "You're chickenshit." I guess they had gotten to feeling mighty comfortable with me, because what ensued was a fight like nothing I've ever witnessed.

I'm embarrassed when people start yelling at each other. I know some of my friends find that funny if not hypocritical, considering what a controversialist I can be, at least in print. I guess I'm inconsistent. Or maybe it's just that I always want to be the one who's making the trouble. Anyway, I was glad to be able to turn back to the stove and get the pasta in and worry about the sauce. "We don't need to put everything in italics," Jonas pleaded. "Punch and Judy—Pierrot and Pierrette—whatever you want to call them—are already the oppressed. They fumble around and beat up on each other because they're not in control of their destinies." Of course that didn't satisfy Jane. "I like italics. Let's italicize everything. I want radical puppets." It turned into an argument about Jonas's mother—the famous bohemian. "I'm sick of your Pierrot and Pierrette fantasy," Jane announced in a voice that was creepily cool. "I hate it when people say we're the perfect couple—just like our puppets. Maybe if your mother hadn't been such a slut you wouldn't always be trying to be such a goody-goody." And then, turning to me, "Marcia, did you know that Jonas freaked out when I wanted to include a scene with Pierrot in the nude?" "I didn't freak out. I just wasn't sure." "You're never sure.

You're not even sure which of your mom's boyfriends paid for you to go to Stanford. Marcia, did you know Jonas doesn't know who his father is?" "And what of it?" "What of it? You're hiding behind your puppets." "But they're your puppets, too." She laughed at this. It was a sarcastic laugh. "What is it you want, Jane, do you want to be the naked puppeteer?" "Sounds good." "Idiot," he muttered.

Jane called the next day to make her apologies. "Sorry. Nobody needs to see one of our fights." I wasn't in a mood for excuses. I'd hardly slept. I hated their screaming. I told myself we all have our demons. Then I wondered why they couldn't keep theirs to themselves. Try as they might, once they'd let me witness one of their own, private Punch and Judy performances there was no going back. Things would be calm for a week and then they'd erupt again. I wasn't seeing anybody at the time—no boyfriend, nobody in my bed. I was laying low and I wasn't minding it. So what did I need with their exhibitionism? From what I gather they've carried on more or less in the same manner. Jane got her way with the swastika and the hammer and sickle. They were just in time for everything to get political. So in a sense she had been right. I think they toured Europe. They're still married. I gather they still have their murderous fights.

9: SUMMER SOLSTICE

A word about fanaticism, extremism, whatever you want to call it. There's a West Coast variety—what I think of as laid-back extremism. That describes Jonas O'Doherty and his vision of the puppet theater as a transcendent game. (Jane was after something else.) Out here the prophets tend to be mystical rather than ideological. Their ideas envelop you, like gongs given a single, soft but penetrating bang. The sound echoes—on and on—in the foggy San Francisco air. Here's the Bay Area philosophy in a nutshell: I'll bang gently on my gong and you'll bang gently on yours. For a hothead like me there can be something weirdly fascinating—soothing, strangely enough—about this West Coast extremism. Am I sounding like an Easterner? Accusing the Westerners of what I guess could be described as anti-intellectualism? Edmund Wilson once wrote, "It is a good deal too easy to be a nihilist on the coast at Carmel: your very negation is a negation of nothing." In other words, there's no pushback, nobody to argue with. Sorry to be sympathizing with Wilson, the prototypical Easterner. I guess I'm a kind of Easterner myself. Maybe all San Francisco Jews are—at heart.

Anyway, in the Bay Area you might as well forget the dialectic. Since everybody's doing their own thing there's no antithesis to be opposed to the thesis and therefore no hope of a synthesis. Nobody out here wants to hear about Plato, Kant, or Hegel. Who can blame them? So why not give Zen or Zoroastrianism a try? Even I, before I got the hell out for a few years, was susceptible, or at least willing to listen. Nothing could have been more oracular than the summer solstice party on the Bolinas Beach that we organized one year, Ginny and I, along with Stuart Smith, a mythomaniacal filmmaker whose fame never went beyond Northern California, and Richard, Stu's poet lover. Richard was tall and handsome, the male sphinx. Stu was the overweight magus. When I say overweight I mean it. But he carried his weight with a comic grandeur. He called himself the Frisco Falstaff—a double joke, since only tourists called San Francisco "Frisco." "You know I was skinny once," I heard him say on more than one occasion. "But not good-looking skinny like Richard, so what the hell was the point? I figured, let's eat." Ginny and I were out at their place in Bolinas for a night in May, still a freezing cold month in Northern California, when we dreamed up that party while sitting in their ramshackle cottage, wind chimes wildly tinkling outside, the general decrepitude disguised, stage set style, by their Salvation Army Art Nouveau finds, candlelight, firelight, dark dirty overstuffed chairs.

I'll never know why we decided to celebrate the summer solstice on a beach where the sun never shines. But in the morning Stu was already designing the invitations as he sat at the table with his coffee and bacon and eggs. Back in SF the next day I had fifty run off and stuffed them in envelopes and there was no turning back. Stu was the oracular filmmaker. Narrative was too much for him. His films—he generally ran out of money after he'd put together fifteen minutes worth—were an onslaught of images, shots of surf on rocks interspersed with sculptures of Hindu gods, that kind of thing. He had some idea about working his movies into our solstice party, with sheets stretched between poles on the beach and three projectors going at once. Double or triple projections were regarded as way out back then, the mother of all of those experiments being the multiple juxtaposed imagines in Abel Gance's *Napoléon*, which somebody had managed to get ahold of and screen for a bunch of us in San Francisco. Stu, a dreamer, died of a massive coronary a few years later. Richard remains devoted. He eventually persuaded the Museum of Modern Art to mount a Stuart Smith evening. Together with a bunch of short films presented in the basement auditorium they managed to put together an unfinished multiscreen work of his, what he called his *Magnum Opus Bucolic*, in the sculpture garden.

I guess it was a memorable party that we organized that summer in Bolinas. It ought to have been, after all the days of frantic preparation. Richard was a pleasant surprise when Ginny and I appeared on Thursday to help out, no longer the quiet, gentle boyfriend we knew. Generally content to sit unobtrusively in a corner, now he was transformed, the sphinx suddenly an impresario, preparing the beach for the solstice feast. He had designed a great pit where the meat, fish, and vegetables would cook for hours deep in the sand. The pit was only the center of what he'd conceived as an earthwork on the theme of the sun, with a dozen rays, each extending six feet, so that the whole ensemble was some fifteen feet wide. Stu had corralled a few of the students from a film class he'd taught, and Richard had them arranging stones by size and color. "We don't even know what it really looks like," Richard announced. "None of us does. We'd have to be hovering somewhere up in the sky to really understand." As for Stu's films, however energetically the students pounded sticks into the ground, they couldn't make them stay put once they'd pulled an old sheet across them; the sheet acted like a sail and the whole structure blew down. "Maybe we can just project the movies on some rocks," Stu said. "I'd like to see what that looks like." But that didn't solve the problem of electricity. Even all the extension cords Stu had collected couldn't get halfway down the hill from the cottage to the beach. Stu had a friend who said he'd bring a generator. But that never happened. That was the end of the movies.

What worried Ginny and me was that there wasn't going to be enough food. We were staying with Stu and Richard, along with Ginny's boyfriend, the union organizer, Giorgio. Ginny was a plain Jane but the exotic guys went for her. Giorgio looked like he was just off the boat from Naples. Actually, he was born and bred in San Francisco. His father had come from Sicily as a kid and somehow managed to get through law school. He was horrified when his son became a union man. As for the food, it worked out. When the beer was running low somebody went off and bought a case of wine. Stu, still disappointed about his movies, emerged not long before the food was finally ready to be dug out of the pit. He was in a sort of caftan, with the scenario for a film about the cosmos inscribed on a long scroll that he had decorated with planets and stars in silver and gold. His text was about passages through time and space and the solar system, with more than a nod to Ouspensky, the Russian mystic who'd been the rage in Paris in the 1920s. Apparently it had taken a generation for San Francisco to hear about Ouspensky; news traveled slow.

"I'm going to climb the ladder to the Moon! Hello Moon!" Stu began. People were so happy to be eating that they didn't really pay much attention as he droned, on and on. "Ladder upon ladder, to Saturn, Mars, Pluto, all the Planets. And then I'm going to climb yet higher, to the Sun! Hello Sun! The Sun is savior, annihilation, renewal." Meanwhile there was another oracular voice, Ginny's Giorgio. I hadn't really noticed a couple of nights earlier, when Giorgio explained that he knew a Latin prayer to the sun, some suspiciously pantheistic text that dated back to the seventeenth century and had nearly gotten the priest who composed it burned at the stake. How did Giorgio know it? He'd learned it from a renegade priest who'd taken a shine to him in the Catholic high school he attended in San Francisco. While Stu stood on the beach offering his oration, Giorgio climbed onto a rock outcropping and offered his Latin prayer. With the fog coming in and out he seemed to be floating on a cloud. He had a good, strong, operatic voice. It must have come in handy at those raucous union meetings. There he was: "Solis! Solis! Solis! Sol est Christus . . ." I suppose it was interesting, a sort of operatic duet, with Stu and Giorgio both singing the praises of the sun that was refusing to shine.

I never really relaxed. I'd been sleeping for two nights on the least comfortable place in the house, the lumpy old Victorian sofa in the living room. Naturally Ginny and Giorgio had the guest room. It was chilly on the beach unless you were close to the fires that Richard had set up at strategic points along the big earthwork, but then you were too hot. I found myself thinking that the party was great, but great in some phony-baloney way. An ex of mine appeared, Burt, a poet and sometime printer of limited edition books. I hadn't seen him in a couple of months. I knew he'd gotten an invitation but somehow hadn't thought he'd appear. "I'm here with Shirley," he said vaguely, nodding in the direction of a thin blond accompanied by a large, handsome dog, as blond as she was. I'd never seen her before. I didn't say anything. "Funny seeing you," he muttered as he took Shirley's hand. I walked off.

Half an hour later I couldn't help but notice Burt and Shirley necking, the two of them somehow in the clinch with that big, handsome caramel colored dog. They were hugging and kissing—and the dog was getting into the act. Burt was between the girl and the dog, reaching his tongue into the dog's mouth, encouraging the dog to stick out its tongue, then turning to Shirley and sticking his tongue in her mouth. Then Burt was licking the dog's muzzle and Shirley was licking the dog and then she was licking Burt, on the lips but all over his face, dog style. A good-looking couple, I had to give them that. And a beautiful dog, although I'm not a dog person. Everybody on the beach was feeling relaxed, but wasn't this taking things a little far? Burt pushed the boundaries. If you challenged him about it he was all gosh-golly-gee. We'd had a bit of a fight after a party at a friend's, where he decided it had gotten a little too warm and sticky and took off his shirt and spent the rest of the evening bare-chested. I can't quite explain it, but there was a guilelessness about his stunts. So what was wrong with French kissing a good-looking dog? Was I feeling some Jewish girl's hang-up about bestiality? Well, light bestiality, anyway.

I was annoyed at myself. But I couldn't help feeling pissed off about Burt, who had no compunction about turning a party I'd organized into a setting for whatever the hell he was up to. I was trying to get Burt and whoever she was out of my mind when I realized that everybody was moving down to the water. There was some kind of commotion. Giorgio had vanished from the rock outcropping. The fog had ebbed and he wasn't there. There had already been arguments about the safety of his going up there and now there were arguments about what we should do. Should somebody climb up and see what was what? And risk another person drowning? "I told him it was reckless." That was Ginny, in a quiet, miserable rage. Stu, ridiculous in his caftan and still holding his scroll, was now reason itself, or so he imagined, though maybe he was the most reckless of all. He had decided that three or four guys should climb up onto the rocks where Giorgio had vanished, but holding onto one another. As if that would prevent them from all being swept to their deaths. There was an argument about how to proceed. And then there was Giorgio, soaked and shivering from head to toe, bleeding from his forehead, walking out of the waves at dusk. He'd slipped, been nearly pulled out by the undertow, but at Saint Xavier's there had been a good swim coach. Giorgio had been on the team. We got him back to the biggest of the fires. Wrapped him in whatever miscellaneous sweaters and blankets were lying around. Ginny was in shock. Burt and the girl didn't seem to have noticed anything. In the darkening distance I saw the two of them kissing—and the dog's tail happily wagging. I think it was later that night, on Stu and Richard's lumpy Victorian sofa, that I decided I was done with San Francisco.

10: LETTERS

Dear Mike,

You know how I feel about my mom. But I've got to thank her (reluctantly—who wants to thank Mom?) for the check that got me to New York. "Go for a month," she said, slipping it into my hand in the kitchen while Dad was reading the *Chronicle* in the living room. "It'll do you good. I don't want you condemned to some crappy secretarial job at the *Chronicle*. It's beneath you. You should be concentrating on your writing." What does she know about it? Anyway, I was done with the *Chronicle* and done with Jane and Jonas and their damn puppet theater. Now I'm wondering if I'll ever go back. I have a cheap sublet on Christopher Street. Great location, true enough, but noisy as hell when the windows are open—and it's summer so there's no alternative. There are nights, with the heat and only one lousy fan, when I might as well be in one of those old social realist novels with desperate people sleeping on fire escapes. But enough bellyaching. The truth is I'm having a damn good time. I think I've hit pay dirt. A couple of days after I arrived I got wind that Allan Kaprow (professor somewhere in New Jersey) was doing one of his Happenings. I thought there might be something to write about. I've been working on it furiously ever since, working harder than I ever have before. And damned if *Harper's* hasn't bought it—for good money, too. They're talking about calling it "Nothing Happening" and giving it the cover in September. Of course you never know. Here's how it opens: "The girl taking money at the door said, 'You won't believe it.' Well, I believe it. The boredom came over me before I'd been in Room #1 for five minutes. I knew there were eight rooms and you were supposed to remain in each one for a full fifteen minutes. Those were the instructions on the program. I felt my life draining away. I tried to hurry into Room #2 but a willowy girl guarding the door stopped me. I was moving too fast. So I had to stay put while a couple, the guy in his underpants and the girl in bra and panties, writhed on the floor. I know it doesn't sound like a big deal. We've all sat through plays that were a hell of a lot longer and didn't have much more to recommend them. But Allan Kaprow's *Eight Rooms* has no lines and no actors, at least no trained actors who might try and make the most of even the lousiest lines. Not that there's any dialogue. *Eight Rooms* suggests a silent movie from hell. I assume the guys and gals involved are all Kaprow's friends, just fucking around." The editor at *Harper's*—maybe you know him, haven't you published there, Mark Landers, more or less our age?—said, "It's perfect. You're giving our readers the facts but also the low-down. They'll love it. You're making them feel as if they're in with the in crowd." Maybe that's my mission. Loads of love, Marcia

Dear Marcia,

I'm glad you've got a mission. Me? I may get run out of town. Maybe I'll join you in that sublet of yours. At the last reading I did—at SF State—a guy, a kid who looked as if he was barely out of high school, yelled at me. My sin? Writing—maybe worse yet reading—sonnets. The damn things barely rhyme. But he picked up on the fourteen lines—smart kid, I guess—and asked what's the point of doing that anymore. Sending love, Mike

Dear Mike,

I've pulled it off—at least for now. I'm staying here. I think I can live on the *Harper's* check for three or maybe four months. Suddenly, since "Nothing Happening" appeared, people are returning my calls. Of course most of the editors barely look up from their desks when you're ushered in for an interview—at least when I'm ushered in. It's not clear they remember why they agreed to see me. When they realize I'm from San Francisco they don't seem to know what to think. Why am I here? Why did I ever want to leave San Francisco? San Francisco is so cool, so they tell me. I had fifteen minutes with Leo Lerman at *Mademoiselle*; everybody agrees he's NYC's answer to Oscar Wilde. He looked at me through eyes magnified by the thickest glasses I've ever seen, presented a full critique of my essay—"brilliant . . . clever . . . well done . . . but are you right? . . . I don't know"—then gave me what at first I thought was a brush-off. "I don't have anything for you right now—the fall season is assigned—but I think I've got an idea that will launch you." He actually said, "Do you know, my dear, you could be enormous." And then: "Do you know about *Spectacles*?

The first issue is appearing soon. I don't know quite when. They have money and they mean to be the newer *New Yorker*—hipper, funnier, tougher, looser. Call this man." He handed me a piece of paper with a name, Max Nelson, and a phone number. I had a drink with Nelson at the Carlyle. He kept saying he loved my ideas. Said he'd be in touch. We'll see. Fingers crossed. Sending love, Marcia

Dear Ginny,
I've met Anaïs Nin. Just what you'd expect. Intolerably mannered. She heard I was in town, called, and invited me to come over to her place. She served tea and you know how I hate tea. We sat at a little table. She started with mutual friends. Soon enough she was my shrink. What are my fantasies? Who do I sleep with? I mentioned Burt and his handpress and that got her going. Turns out she had a lover, Gonzalo, South American, I think, who for several years was supposed to be in charge of the press she bought to print her little books. A guy with a printing press was going to be our bond, so she imagined. "What is it about men and their machines?" she asked. She complained that when it came to it she did most of the printing. Gonzalo had been in love with the mystique of their little press but hadn't done anything much about it. He was lazy. "And your lover?" she asked. That was none of her goddamn business. Love to you, Marcia

Dear Mike,
The discussions with the people who are starting *Spectacles* drag on. I've met with them three times. It started with Max Nelson—I think I mentioned him—and now there are three other guys, two editors

and somebody who's going to be the designer, at least I think that's what's going on. We meet for lunch—long, drawn-out lunches—and everything goes around in circles. Two were at Del Pezzo, where conversations never get very far because everybody's so busy saying hello to the people at the other tables. I'm told this was where Le Corbusier hung out when he was working on the UN building. They say they're starting the magazine early in the new year but don't seem sure. Everything I suggest is enthusiastically embraced and then by the next time we meet there's a problem. Or I suggest something and somebody says, "Oh, wasn't so-and-so talking about that?" About doing it for the magazine? Or just about it? They seem to like the idea of my starting—if I ever get the job—with something attacking San Francisco. "Forgetting Frisco" is what they like as a title. The gist would be that *Evergreen Review*'s "San Francisco Scene" issue made too much of SF. Frankly, I don't think they know what *Spectacles* is supposed to be . . . except a big success. They've figured out that I don't have a philosophical bone in my body. They like that. There was some talk about asking Dwight Macdonald to write something but Max shot that down, saying, "Dwight can't get that old dialectical reasoning out of his head. Whatever he says he sounds like a fucking Marxist, with his on-the-one-hand-on-the-other-hand." They've definitely taken a shine to the idea that I would have no specific beat. I'll write about film, music, theater, art, do reviews, profiles, travel pieces, as if all the distinctions were in disarray and we'd been left to fend for ourselves. "Look at Socrates," Max said at some point. "What was his 'beat'?" I wasn't sure whether this was meant as a joke or a brilliant remark. Well, there you have it. Sending love, Marcia

Hi Mike,

I've been hired. $175 a week—fantastic. I met the main backer—or backers, father and son. That gave me pause. The father is in the rag trade. Made a fortune with clothes for boys and girls headed to summer camp. A whole line. The concept, so he explains, makes it a cinch for Mom to outfit Dick and Jane for the Catskills. The son is in the business but of course wants to expand, move up in the world; he has a BA from Harvard and some other degree from Yale. He wants to compete with *The New Yorker*—which he says everybody thinks is old hat. Do they have any idea how tough it's going to be? I worry. But I'm thrilled. First issue is in February. The plan is to experiment a bit in the deep winter months when, so Max believes, everybody is still too hungover from the holidays to pay much attention. Come next fall all the kinks will have been worked out and the conquest of Manhattan will begin. The advertisers seem to be coming on board. After going around in circles my opening piece is going to be "Forgetting Frisco." I'm a little nervous. Talk about making enemies. The point is that the avant-garde community, in SF or anywhere else, is dead and gone if it ever existed in the first place. Avant-gardism—the great communal dream—was always a phantasm. Now it's everybody for himself—or herself. Sending love, Marcia

Hello Ginny,

Sorry to be out of touch. The magazine—*Spectacles*—is taking off. I've spent most of this week with the designer. He seems to run the show and has all kinds of fancy plans for my first piece, wrapping text around images or creating a double page spread with a checkerboard of little photographs and text interspersed. Will it work? Will anybody be able to read the damn thing? The subject? San Francisco. A sort of sour take, I'm a little embarrassed to say. But what I really wanted to tell you was that I thought of you the other day when I saw a show of Navajo rugs at one of the better uptown galleries. They generally show contemporary abstract painting. And then this. One of the rugs looked just like the red, brown, and gray one you have in the corner of your living room. Sending love, Marcia

11: *SLUMMINGS*

I didn't see Marcia again until 1963, when she appeared in the Bay Area on tour for *Slummings*, her first and only essay collection. When I say I saw her I mean just that. We exchanged no more than six or seven words at the party Mike threw for her, a fancy affair with fantastic food paid for by her publisher—so Mike, who didn't like to spend money, assured me. "Hey, you!" Marcia said as I approached. She was deep in conversation with somebody. I can't remember who. I've never been a big talker and couldn't manage much in response. "Good to see you. Congratulations. Great book." That was all I got out before she dismissed me with a big smile and turned back to whomever it was she was talking to.

Mike's party was after her reading at the California School of Fine Arts—which by then had been renamed the San Francisco Art Institute. That was a mob scene, standing room only. I can't say I was surprised. The book had been reviewed everywhere. *Time* magazine declared Marcia "a new kind of critic, more interested in her own feelings than whatever she's loving or hating. What Randall Jarrell called 'the age of criticism' is turning into the age of narcissism. Love her or hate her, Marcia Lang may turn out to be the voice of the new decade. She's all of forty years old." Everybody in San Francisco wanted to get a look at the hometown girl who'd made good in New York. Walking onto the stage she seemed a little stunned at the size of the crowd. Though it wasn't necessarily as large as it looked. After all, the auditorium isn't that big. I could see that momentary hard look in Marcia's blue eyes, the look she got when she was caught off guard and was busy getting herself back on track. But this was a new Marcia, carefully groomed, wearing a dressed-for-success matching jacket and skirt. "Wow," she began. "I'm sure as hell excited to be back here."

Marcia was all business. She read for maybe fifteen minutes from her takedown of Bertolt Brecht. "I'm sick of polemics," she began. "Isn't everybody sick of polemics? And I'm sick to death of the bright, cold white light that bathes the new Brecht productions. In their own way those klieg lights are as bland and banal as the shadow play that was all the rage among avant-garde theater groups before the war." Marcia sounded both pissed off and exhilarated. She knew she had people squirming. After all, they loved Brecht—or at least they thought they should. Marcia was definitely in her element during the question and answer period, laughing off friendly comments and cheerfully dismissing frankly hostile questions. It was the Marcia I'd known around the old oak table when we were living together. There was the same easy energy, disarming you even as she dismissed you. Only now it was projected on a much bigger scale. Somehow she made everybody in the audience feel they were on intimate terms with her, even when she was making them uncomfortable. When somebody embarked on a point-by-point critique of her critique of Brecht, she patiently waited for her to finish and then, before answering, said, "Do you mind if I ask you a question?" "No. Of course not." "You're wild about *Mother Courage*, right?" The answer was yes. Which enabled Marcia to evade the larger question, about Brecht's politics, and plunge straight into a takedown of *Mother Courage*. "Brecht's women are the worst kind of clichés. He insists on his clichés—in this case the long-suffering mother dressed up as an existential comedian—or is it tragedian? I think he hates women."

I bought *Slummings* the day it came out, which isn't my style. I tend to wait for books to appear on a remainder table. But I figured it was the least I could do after the six or eight months I'd lived in her apartment rent free. I hadn't seen most of the theater, music, and art she was writing about—I don't get to New York—but there was something about her resistance to specialization and her willingness to go off on tangents that felt like a San Francisco thing. Here and there she reminisced about her Bay Area days. I liked that. I especially love her piece about Art Nouveau, precipitated by the big show at the Museum of Modern Art in 1960, but winding back to people and places we shared. "I have a Tiffany Wisteria lamp hanging over the table as I'm writing this." That was the opening line. "True, it has a couple of missing pieces. But beggars can't be choosers. And it was—what? five bucks?—in one of the Salvation Army stores in San Francisco in 1951. Of course that was a lot of money. A few years out of college, my friends and I were fascinated by Art Nouveau. Fascinated and ambivalent. We didn't know what to make of it. We didn't know whether to love or hate the stuff: the fainting Ophelia on an ashtray of imitation bronze; the drooping table lamp with the purple glass shade shaped like a flower; the porcelain vase that suggested a volcanic explosion (some of the little flames annoyingly chipped). I'm still not sure. Is this stuff dreamlike or dreary? Visionary or merely murky?"

Marcia accused the Museum of Modern Art of sanitizing Art Nouveau, betraying its uneasy spirit. "In theory I'm happy about the Modern's show," she declared. "But the truth is that the museum is distorting Art Nouveau, co-opting the movement for its own purist purposes. That's where the trouble begins. They've taken the sex and *schmaltz* out of Art Nouveau. They've set every last necklace, lamp, and poster against the starkest imaginable backdrop. This is Art Nouveau cleaned up, ready for a Madison Avenue ad campaign. Actually, I think I've already seen a couple of those ads in *The New Yorker*. The Modern show is Art Nouveau for grinds, not hipsters. I'm not saying the hipsters really understand Beardsley, Gaudí, Mackintosh, or Guimard, but I'm not sure that Peter Selz, who organized the show, does either." Art Nouveau, Marcia argued, was an anti-mainstream movement, with cottage industry geniuses operating in Barcelona, Brussels, Glasgow. Cities, in other words, beyond the two or three main metropolises of the late nineteenth century. She came right out and said that Art Nouveau flourished in places a little like the San Francisco of her youth. "That's why my North Beach friends were fascinated by Art Nouveau," she wrote. "It was a movement that exploded at the margins—in places like San Francisco. Now here's

New York City's Museum of Modern Art taking it over—mainstreaming it, denying its quirky and maybe even queasy poetry." Her last line was this: "You can't understand an Art Nouveau ashtray until you've stubbed out a cigarette—or, better yet, a joint—on Ophelia's bronzed boobs."

But what most incited the reviewers of *Slummings* was Marcia's slash-and-burn job on Brecht. This was more than a takedown of the theatrical avant-garde. Marcia was going after a lot of her old Lefty friends from Berkeley days when she argued that behind Brecht the humanitarian there was a dyed-in-the-wool Stalinist. Although the piece was called "Why I Hate Brecht," she began quietly enough. Seducing readers before socking it to 'em was one of Marcia's talents. She acknowledged the glory of *The Threepenny Opera* and its long run at the Theatre de Lys in Greenwich Village. "But was *The Threepenny Opera* really Brecht's achievement?" she asked. "Or course not. Just imagine it without Kurt Weill's music and Lotte Lenya's singing. What would we be left with? Nothing!" This brought her to the hook of her piece, the theatrical evening called *Brecht on Brecht* that had been mounted at the de Lys more or less concurrently with the closing days of *The Threepenny Opera*'s run. "People arrive at the de Lys with warm feelings for *The Threepenny Opera*," she began. "They're predisposed to enjoy themselves. George Tabori, who arranged these bits and pieces of Brecht, takes you right up to the edge of Brecht's Leftist posturing. Then he pulls away. There's a mocking section about the idea of freedom. 'Freedom all around!' an actor declaims. 'Freedom for everybody! Freedom for warmongers! Freedom for exploiters! Freedom for Krupp and freedom for Eichmann!' Just when you're beginning to feel hectored and lectured with these histrionic ironies the spotlight moves to another skilled actor—or there's Lenya to sing a song. It's a Brechtian gabfest—a cocktail party of an evening at the theater."

"*Brecht on Brecht*," she pursued, "has enough fashionable nihilistic trimmings to persuade the skeptical postwar audience to feel a little sentimental about the old Marxist romance. All I can say is that it's all well and good to have Galileo announcing that 'the only purpose of science is to lighten the toil of human existence.' But doesn't that sound more than a little like the Leninists and Stalinists with their science of society?" When the Brecht piece first appeared in *Spectacles*—and later, when it was reprinted in *Slummings*—people said Marcia's citations from *Galileo* and *Mother Courage* were so selective as to amount to fraud. "Behind Brecht's tough facade," she wrote, "there's an obfuscatory authoritarian. What could be worse? Isn't this the ultimate totalitarian mentality?" One reviewer said that Marcia Lang tossed around words like Marxist and totalitarian without the faintest idea what they really meant. Marcia was unrepentant. A few years later, when we were living together, she told me she felt vindicated by rumors circulating in New York that Sidney Hook, the ex-Marxist, had heard Brecht defend Stalin's executions of Grigory Zinoviev and Lev Kamenev, two men who'd been close to Lenin. "The more innocent they are, the more they deserve to be shot," Brecht had supposedly told Hook. Marica loved to hate that line of Brecht's.

12: *AND THEN THERE WERE NONE . . .*

Dear Mike,

Well here I am in Rome, living with Simon in a great apartment on the Via dei Foraggi. I knew Simon in New York and he jumped at the chance to come along. What can I tell you about him? He's an intellectual lounge lizard, if that makes any sense. Had a few mid-level editorial jobs but was too casual to ever get anywhere, at least that's my impression. He's fine. Anyway I'm up to my ears writing about the preparations for *And Then There Were None . . .*, the totally insane evening being arranged at the Opera House. I haven't seen that much of Simon. I'm having the time of my life. The photographs for the feature are being taken by Ugo Mulas. Do you know the name? Fabulous Italian guy. Dramatic but casual black-and-white photographs. As for Simon. He seems content. He's hooked up with some people at the American Academy who are fascinated, so he tells me, by his never-ending—and, I believe, never-to-be-finished—book about centaurs. I can't really make out what he sees in them (I meant the centaurs, but I guess I also mean the scholars at the Academy).

The other day he was excited about a sugar packet he'd picked up at some café, emblazoned with a centaur wearing a chef's hat. "The endurance of an image," he explained as if he were Erwin Panofsky. Anyway, mostly he's languid and stubborn, and after thinking about him as Not-so-simple Simon—no secret, I've called him that to his face—I'm beginning to think of him as the Roman roué, not that I think he's really up to anything much.

But enough about Simon. Let's talk about Rome. You may think I'm crazy but Rome reminds me of San Francisco. I'd say Rome is San Francisco with a history, a hyperbolic San Francisco, SF on steroids. Of course there's the physical aspect, the hills, the ups and downs, the smashing vistas. I think I could make the argument that Borromini's crazy architecture is San Francisco Victorian gingerbread, only taken to the heights—transcendent gingerbread. I wouldn't dare say any of this in print. Or maybe I will. You never know. Maybe what I'm feeling is that Rome in its old age has collapsed into a second childhood that's a little like San Francisco, which has never gotten past its childhood as the promising Pacific Coast metropolis. I'm talking about a provincial cosmopolitanism. Or is it a cosmopolitan provincialism? In New York, London, and Paris they still believe in a center, the imperial city. Of course Rome *was* the imperial city. But that was a long time ago. New Yorkers imagine that San Franciscans envy them their centrality. I know there's a lot of that. But there's also something to be said for decentralization. Instead of the overarching order and standards of New York, London, or Paris, you have neighborhoods, fiefdoms, little rival magazines, alleys, tangents. Zen, collage, meditation, gamelan music, eccentricity in all its variety. So where does this leave you and your poetry? I don't know.

Do you ever actually see *Spectacles*? Anyway, I'm enclosing a draft of the first few pages of my piece. I'm excited about it. It will be something like seven thousand words in the magazine and then expanded to twenty thousand or so for the book, which is going to be called *A Night at the Opera*, with the text running amid Ugo's fantastic photographs. Sending love, Marcia

"A Night at the Opera"
by Marcia Lang

Only a madman could imagine pulling off something like *And Then There Were None . . .*—and Giovanni Carandente, the Italian art critic, curator, and cultural impresario with the roundest face and the biggest smile you've ever seen is definitely the man for the job. I have no idea how he managed to corral Italo Calvino to dream up a scenario, Pierre Boulez to write the music, and an international cavalcade of artists including Saul Steinberg, Emilio Vedova, Niki de Saint Phalle, Ellsworth Kelly, Jean Tinguely, Jean Arp, and Nam June Paik to design the seven segments through which a soprano and a tenor wander in search of . . . what . . . oh, it doesn't really matter. Calvino, the most elegant of men, speaks of a fairy tale for our time. When I ask him how it's all supposed to add up he offers one of his charming shrugs and after a few moments smiles and responds, "But why should our time add up?" The scenario was supposed to conclude with the seven separate settings by seven different artists somehow merging before they vanished, leaving the poor tenor and soprano to do . . . what . . . nobody seems sure. Boulez hasn't quite finished the score and apparently he and Calvino have never exactly agreed as to how the story, such as it is, is meant to resolve. Anyway, close coordination is out of the question, with the artists appearing and disappearing from the US, France, Switzerland, and who knows where else, even as the team at the Opera is trying to build the sets and prepare for rehearsals. In the face of all this Carandente just smiles. When I ask him if the evening was inspired by Pirandello's *Six Characters in Search of an Author* he responds, "Oh, it's much bigger than that." Did I mention that Glen Tetley and Jerry Robbins are rumored to be providing some choreography? Though neither has yet appeared. And the premiere is weeks away.

As of this moment the extravaganza will have but two showings at the Rome Opera House and maybe never be seen again. That's fine with Carandente, who seems enchanted by the idea of "impermanence," as he puts it. Among the many mysteries surrounding this extravaganza is who on earth is footing the bill. Carandente won't say. The project manager just looks at me, poker-faced, when I ask. But the rumors are that somebody in the Agnelli family is romantically involved with the soprano and is pouring money into this madness. Of course the artists claim that they're barely being paid. Everybody's doing it for the love of it. Or for immortality. Or maybe just for a free trip to Rome. Carandente has Alitalia covering the airfare.

Ellsworth Kelly, who's designed a dozen big flat color shapes (rectangles and triangles) that perform a sort of dance, told me he came on board because he heard that Arp was participating. I gather Arp, who appeared in Rome for only a day, instructed Carandente to tear a hundred newspapers into bits and pieces and have them dropped from the top of the theater onto the stage. "It's like the old days at the Café Voltaire during World War I, when Sophie and I had just met," he cheerfully remarked, Sophie being Sophie Taeuber-Arp, the gifted artist who was his wife and died in 1943; her geometric abstractions, still not well known in the United States, are having a vogue over here. Nam June Paik, who's piling television sets in a labyrinth for the soprano to navigate, says he's doing it because Tinguely agreed. Paik, when I spoke with him, waxed enthusiastic about Tinguely's sensational evening at the Museum of Modern Art in New York a few years back, when his self-destructing sculpture did its thing—or at least tried to. "If Jean thinks this is where it's at," Paik explained, "this is where I am."

As for Vedova, the Italian Abstract Expressionist, he plans to perform himself, turning his cubicle into a three-dimensional painting, slapping the paint around in front of the audience as the two singers sing a duet. He's going to be the embodiment of Harold Rosenberg's action painter, only finally realized in Italy. Saul Steinberg, who's actually a friend of Rosenberg's, has ended up staying in Rome for months—Carandente seems a little worried about how to pay his hotel bill—creating an elaborate reconstruction of Rome on the four walls of the cubicle he's been given to design. "Does it all go together?" I ask Carandente. "Of course not," he responds with his biggest smile, "that's the point."

Dear Mike,

Here's one of the first copies of *A Night at the Opera*—for you, my dear friend. I hope you like it, if not what I've written, then at least for Ugo's wonderful photographs. Those blurred black-and-white shots of the preparations probably capture it all a lot better than I have. Sorry if I sound bummed out. But it seems to be turning out that writing about *And Then There Were None* . . . is the prelude to there being no place for me in Old New York. Have you heard? No, probably not, you poets don't follow the media talk. (Ha!) *Spectacles* is going belly-up. I returned from Rome to an almost empty office. Next month will be the last issue. It seems that the father and son team who were funding it weren't on the same page—which I half suspected from the beginning. The response to the magazine has been terrific, but they've been losing money every month. Junior believed they had to expand in order to make a go of it, while with each passing issue senior was more convinced that his son with the Ivy League education was a dummy. My initial reaction to the end of my paycheck was a weird exhilaration. I figured I'd made enough money to coast for a few months. And wouldn't another magazine give me a job? After all, *Slummings* has been the talk of the town. But it's been strange. I think I'm regarded as some kind of fly-by-night phenomenon, the smart-alecky gal from *Spectacles*—and yes it was fun while she was doing her thing—but now it's goodbye and good riddance. So I'm thinking of returning to SF, with my tail between my legs or not, it all depends on how you think about it. Sending love, Marcia

Dear Ginny,

Well, Simon has left. Went off to London with a bitch by the name of Suzy Grand. Things haven't been good since we got back from Rome. I've hardly noticed, I've been so busy getting *A Night at the Oper*a ready for the magazine and then straight into the book. And then there's the collapse of *Spectacles*. My career on the rocks. You may see me back in San Fran any day now. But back to Not-so-simple Simon and his exit. Our Roman apartment was just the right setting for Simon. You should have seen him hovering over the little cocktail table, Mr. Know-It-All with the weird Italian aperitifs he'd discovered in some shop in Trastevere. Since our return he's been grumpy about the Upper West Side, not that he's done anything about it. What can he do? He's a grifter. I shouldn't complain. But wouldn't you think he could at least replace a broken toilet seat? His specialty is sliding into people's beds and living rooms. First mine. Now Suzy's. Did I tell you about Suzy? London dealer and curator, always talking up kinetic art—Vasarely, that Venezuelan guy Soto, and I don't know who else. She's a fat pig of a gal. Well, maybe not fat. Just plump. Looks like an overstuffed ottoman when she's in one of her trendy outfits. But who am I to talk? My weight has been going up as I've sat here writing this damn Roman thing. And panic over losing my paycheck hasn't helped. I suppose in Simon's mind—does he ever really think?—Suzy and I are more or less the same quantity, overweight pushers and shovers who need him to class up the joint. I'm making it sound too calculating. With Simon it's instinct, pure or impure I can't really say. Sending love, Marcia

13: MARIN

I still have the printing press in San Francisco. I stay there for a few days every couple of weeks, sleeping on the daybed. Mostly I'm here in Marin. For me the house, the house Marcia left me, is a big deal. A place to live in comfort. I don't plan to leave. If for some reason things get bad—health issues are what we all worry about—I might just jump off the balcony and roll down the ravine and never be seen or heard from again. Perfect setting for the death of an obscure middle-aged poet and publisher. I still set type by hand.

Marcia always needed a setting. This fit the bill. Call it the house that Lang Fine Wines and Spirits built. Guests, after struggling to park their cars on the ridiculously narrow street, would let out a gasp as they stumbled down the steep steps into Marcia's five or six redwood rooms (depends on how you count). The structure is set on huge redwood stilts. "It was designed by Dick Grossman and he built it with his own two hands," she announced when I came down the steps the first time. I was with Stan, a mutual friend. He'd given me a ride from the city. "You remember Dick from the old days," she went on before I'd had a chance to get a word in. "The house is sheer genius if you're into the last gasps of the Arts and Crafts movement." "Are you?" I asked. She gave me a quick look. I'd caught her. She wasn't prepared to be grilled about the Arts and Crafts movement. "Oh, it's something," she came back, giving me a hug. "Anyway, it was a bargain." So we began again. I guess I was the bullshit detector who liked her bullshit. I've concluded that she liked it that way.

Of course the house was a bargain. The place had been falling apart practically since Dick and his wife moved in. Anybody who was into fine Japanese-style carpentry knew that Dick Grossman was a screw-up. He was no Nakashima. He was no Noguchi, though people said he'd studied with him. He had been determined to build the house, at least some of the house, out of timber from the redwoods that had to be taken down before work could begin. The problem, at least one of the problems, was that Dick never let the wood properly cure. He didn't know what he was doing. He was impatient. Dick's Japanese jigsaw joints were sloppy. Clots of hardened glue ruined what were meant to be elegant corners. And he used all kinds of metal brackets and braces that no self-respecting woodworker would have touched. The staircase leading up to the bedrooms was great to look at but not so great when you took a few steps and discovered that the structure was shaking. The same was true for the sort of catwalk that functioned as an upstairs hallway, connecting the stairs with the bedrooms and Marcia's study. The impressive looking fireplace, the first piece of stonework that Dick had attempted, leaked smoke and soot and had almost immediately been replaced by a Vermont cast-iron stove that stood incoherently in front of what I gather

Dick's wife referred to as Dicky's rock pile. The place was impossible for people with kids. When Dick and his wife died within months of each other their son didn't want anything to do with it. For god's sake he'd grown up here. There isn't much privacy and you're always in danger of losing somebody if they step out of the French doors that in each of the bedrooms open onto a rickety little balcony. Marcia kept the French doors in our bedroom and her study permanently locked. Like many reckless people she was a worrywart when it came to certain safety measures. But she couldn't bring herself to do anything about the perilous rustic railings, a lacework of twigs and branches that Dick had designed for the staircase and the catwalk. They're a big part of the house's crazy charm.

In daylight, to be honest, the place sometimes looks as if it's coming apart at the seams. You can almost hear the cracks widening in the buckling redwood walls. Luckily, there isn't much daylight, between the redwoods and the fog. As for the house at night, that's a whole other story. The high ceiling is damn dramatic, with Marcia's cheap Japanese lanterns creating interesting shadow patterns here and there. It isn't your usual peaked ceiling, but a conglomeration of cubes, something about atomic structure, an idea Dick picked up from a seminar with Bucky Fuller. There are a bunch of ninety-degree angles and mysterious recesses. The two bedrooms and the study upstairs are cubes cut into the main cube. And then there's the staircase and the catwalk connecting the upstairs rooms, all of it framed by Dick's nifty but treacherous twig-and-branch railings. At certain moments, from certain angles, the house suggests one of Piranesi's architectural fantasies, with Roman stone and stucco replaced by California redwood. I can't say I've entertained much since Marcia died, but when I do I try Marcia's technique of handing guests a glass of wine even before they've had a chance to notice how weird the place really is—weird or weirdly interesting, depending on your idea of home sweet home. When she had a party I held back and let her get things rolling. Even after I had pretty much sublet my place in the city, she treated me like—I don't know how to describe it—not exactly a guest, but a sidekick, somewhat tentatively. Which was fine with me, since in a way I've always felt temporary—uncertain about my status. It was that way the first time around with Marcia, when we were seniors at Berkeley, and the second time around, when she was working that lousy job at the *Chronicle* and we lived together for much of a year.

I guess this will always be Marcia's place. But I got to know the area a lot better than she did. She never stepped out the front door, except when we were going to dinner, a party, or something in the city. I can't blame her. She didn't know how to drive and there wasn't anywhere to walk even if there had been some sidewalks. Why she bought this crazy house in the first place I never really understood. She said she'd always meant to learn to drive. I don't believe it. Anyway, within six months of buying Dick Grossman's folly—that was what she called it after paying one too many handyman's bills—we'd reconnected and I was her driver. I could do without the driving. I'm happier on my bike. That's how I've always gotten around San Francisco. While Marcia was alive I made some kind of bicycle excursion nearly every day. Got me out of the house. Sometimes it was just the mile to the little general store for milk or eggs. Two or three times a week, at least when the weather was good, I'd go off for a couple of hours, winding up steep roads, avoiding the cars that whizzed around blind corners, my lungs full of cold, clean air. When I got back to the house, there would be Marcia, stretched out on the couch exactly where I'd left her, or so it seemed. "You again," was her line, said ironically but fondly. I can't say my routine has changed much since that night at the Opera.

But right now I'm in Marcia's study. I guess you could say it's my study now, up the rickety staircase and along the rickety catwalk, right next to our bedroom. I'm sorry if I've gotten into too many details about the house. Can't help it. It's my practical bent. After years working with an old, balky printing press I'm a little obsessed with the way things do or don't work. I do think it's nifty how the cubic profiles of the study and the bedrooms hang over—and, really, cut into—the big living room, defining the lower ceilings of the kitchen and the dining area. Marcia called it Dick's West Coast Cubism. Right she was. Dick was a lousy craftsman but he had a hell of an eye. It's pretty spectacular up here in her study. Marcia had her chair and desk arranged so that when she worked she faced the view out the back of the house. What a view! There's a steep drop behind the house, covered with some spectacularly ancient, twisted live oaks. They look as if they're hanging on for dear life. Beyond that are more mountains, disappearing and reappearing as the fog moves in and out.

Marcia's manuscripts are in folders in the big deep drawers of this desk. The archivists at Berkeley asked me to "preserve Miss Lang's organization," though I can't see much order. When I was first going through whatever she'd left of this unfinished manuscript I wondered if she'd written about me. There are a few things, which is somehow a relief and somehow an insult. Of course she's right about that time on the beach in Bolinas when I was making out with Shirley and Shirley's dog. I'll admit I was aware I was pissing Marcia off. That was part of the fun. Anyway, who knows how Marcia planned to put everything together. Some of the people she wrote about I would've expected. But Nick? That surprised me. I wouldn't have imagined she even noticed him. Marcia could be brutal. But she was also cynical about her own brutality. That was her saving grace. And—maybe it's not so surprising—she was becoming sentimental about the old San Francisco that in our youth we'd never given a second thought. Amid the notes scribbled on bits of paper I found this: "Try to use a line from Dos Passos's *Manhattan Transfer*. 'Yessir these aint the champagne suppers we used to have in Frisco in the ole days.'" One of the longest sections she completed—at least there's a full draft—is about a fin de siècle fellow by the name of Gelett Burgess, the mastermind behind a short-lived San Francisco magazine, *The Lark*.

There are notes for something about the Moss Beach Distillery, in Half Moon Bay, just south of San Francisco on the coast, where we sometimes ended up in the late 1940s. It depended on somebody having a car. "Imagine," she wrote, "a Prohibition era gin joint still operating after World War II—a place out of time—and you have some sense of the fascination that the Moss Beach Distillery exerted on our disreputable crew. The dark dirt road up the cliff to the ramshackle place was always a challenge, with its murderous hairpin turns. Even if we were trying to arrive before sundown the fog was so thick that all you could see was the gleam of your own headlights, like something in a film noir. We loved the damn place, set on a rock outcropping. It felt like the end of the earth. When we'd finally parked and stepped in we were back in the 1920s or 1930s. There were always a few old guys sitting at the dusty bar. One of them claimed to be related to Gertrude, Leo, and Michael Stein, a first or second cousin from their Bay Area years. Then there were the tables with local couples out for an evening. There was a minimal menu: chili, burgers, fish and chips. The décor was no-décor, aside from a few paintings, not the worst paintings, hanging here and there. There was always the crashing sound of the surf. And if the moon was out and the fog gave you a chance, you could see the surf curling and fragmenting as it hit the rocks, a Hokusai or Hiroshige print come to life. The atmosphere was warm and damp, even if the night was cool. We loved the Moss Beach Distillery. We were high on the place even before we'd ordered a couple of pitchers of beer."

When I first read this I was amazed to find Marcia in such a romantic mood. There are a few passages in the manuscript where she herself seems to confess to being amazed. As I said at the outset, I have no idea how she was planning to put together all these pages that I've found in her files. I don't think she knew herself. She seems to have written about things as they came to her. Here are a couple of pieces that I can't figure out what to do with. I tried starting the book with the essay about Gelett Burgess and fin de siècle San Francisco, but that didn't feel right. So I've stuck it in here, followed by something about a couple who arrived from New York and . . . well—she describes what happened then. After which I think I'm pretty much done.

14: GELETT BURGESS

"You'd like his stuff, Marcia," a friend said to me, "Ambrose Bierce is Barbary Coast Dada." Maybe so. But what did I need with Bierce when half of my Berkeley friends were Dadaists? When I was at Berkeley in the 1940s I was uncomfortable with the old bohemian San Francisco. I never read Bierce or Bret Harte or the rest of the long-gone local literati. Still haven't. I know people think some of the writing's really good. But to us the old San Francisco—the gold rush saloons, the Barbary Coast brothels—was a big, dumb cliché. Just thinking about the tourists lining up in North Beach to get a look at whatever was left of the city's sins made my flesh crawl.

What was worse was that in the 1940s some of the old bohemians were still around, remnants of the 1920s, crumbling but ambulatory, dreamers and schemers long past their expiration dates. When a bunch of us splurged on dinner at Vanessi's or Finocchio's in North Beach—the food was good—I couldn't help but cringe at some doddering old couple sitting at a table in a corner. The Barbary Coast legends still make me uneasy. My sense is that it was never more than a pale echo of the old la vie bohème, the Parisian original reheated, and who's to say that the original amounted to more than a bunch of middle class poseurs? But I have a problem. Thinking about it now it seems to me that we were, like that earlier generation, in almost equal parts authentic, artificial, and absurd. Which gives me some sympathy for the old farts and all *their* ambiguities. When our gang gets together I look around and I begin to suspect that if you gave us another twenty or thirty years we'd look like those geezers at Vanessi's. And of course I can't forget that when I was in my twenties I was sort of seduced by one of them—Cal Cummings—who at the time wasn't so terribly much older than I am now.

Anyway, lately I've found myself poking around in some of the books the old timers wrote, things so cheap in those cavernous old downtown used bookstores that I couldn't resist buying them decades ago, even if I had no intention of reading them. Now I'm wondering if there was all that much of a rupture between them and us—or any rupture at all. Which brings me to Gelett Burgess and *The Lark*, a man and a magazine that represented everything I hated about fin de siècle San Francisco and now find myself reconsidering with a certain fondness or even a shock of recognition. Maybe it's living with Burt—who, like Gelett, publishes a little magazine with funny typography—that makes me now warm to this kind of literary nonsense. I have to confess that I've grown fond of Burt's mag—he calls it *Velocipede*, although I still think he'd be smart to get rid of some of those Victorian typefaces. "It's elegant kitsch," he once said in his defense. To which I responded that there was no such thing. I find myself wondering if Gelett was at all like Burt—although in some respects Gelett was more like me.

When he died in 1951 *The New York Times* remembered Burgess for his most famous verse, "The Purple Cow," a bit of late Victorian nonsense that seems to have endured, I can't say why. Call it sub-Lewis Carroll.

> I never saw a Purple Cow,
> I never hope to see one,
> But I can tell you, anyhow,
> I'd rather see than be one!

You get the drift. Burgess was born in Boston in 1866. He studied at the Massachusetts Institute of Technology, headed west for a job as a draftsman with the Southern Pacific Railroad, and went on to teach topographical drawing at UC Berkeley. (Me? I came from somewhere else, too. Born in Germany to parents who left in the nick of time.) One night in 1894 Burgess found himself, along with a couple of buddies, pulling down a statue of a temperance crusader by the name of Dr. Henry D. Cogswell on the corner of Market and California. To Burgess and his friends, the Cogswell statue was a pompous joke, with an outstretched hand that conveniently functioned as a drinking fountain, offering water to the city's sober citizens. They believed it had to go. Burgess, the naughty boy, was forced to resign from his Berkeley job. He later recalled that in their "hair-brained Youth" he and his buddies wanted to "demolish Decadence." A decadent who wanted to demolish decadence. I like that.

"It is a very laboratory of melodrama," Burgess wrote about San Francisco at the end of his life, when he was living in Carmel. (And here I am, lying low in Marin County.) About the melodrama of San Francisco I can't disagree. There's this big little city thing about San Francisco, the petty feuds of a Peyton Place, but overplayed and overdetermined. San Francisco is charming but also schizoid. I think that's what Burgess was getting at when he said that San Francisco "is a little cosmos, bizarre, isolate, remote, all things to all men, wrapped in a variegated mantle of chance and change." There's something delusional about the city—delusions of importance, delusions of seriousness, when really everybody is a nervous wreck. Here's Burgess again: "Interwoven in her domestic life are strange threads of local pride, and fetish-worship of the established centres of the world's culture." You can say that again. One thing I really hate about San Francisco is the never-ending ambivalence about New York. No, whatever you are, you're not New York City. I should know. I like that Burgess was good at hate. He hated the gingerbread architecture, which makes me smile now that everybody reveres those damn Victorian homes. "Architectural shams," he called them. "It would be hard to select the prize monstrosity," he wrote of the new houses; "it should be a restless, uncertain, frightful collection of details, giving the effect of a nightmare about to explode." Tell that to the real estate agents and doctors and lawyers who are buying up the Victorians and spending a fortune restoring the gingerbread! Was Burgess a purist of a sort? I see that he published an attack on "the abuse of adjectives" titled "The Decrescence of Purism." I guess I'm one of the abusers, at least I've been accused of that.

Burgess both ribbed and (obviously) revered the little magazines that were being published around 1900, among them Paris's *La*

Revue blanche, London's *The Yellow Book*, and Chicago's *The Chap-Book*. "The craze for 'fad magazines,'" he later wrote, "('fadazines,' we called them) was at its high noon." His biggest contribution to the craze was *The Lark*, published monthly in 1896 and 1897, twenty-five issues in all, on a strange dark paper made of bamboo that Burgess and his pals discovered in some Chinatown warehouse; the paper has held up remarkably well. Years ago I picked up a beat-up bound copy of one of the years, with a cover design featuring a minimally dressed fellow sitting cross-legged playing a flute. When I told my buddy Ray Lewis, who runs a local gallery specializing in prints by the modern masters, that I was interested in *The Lark*, he gave me the other volume (apparently there are only two), this one with another young fellow, identified as Marsyas, playing a mouth organ. It's a perfect copy, nothing but the best for Ray. Among the contributors to *The Lark* was the poet Yone Noguchi, the father of the sculptor, although they never had much to do with each other. Yone was a son of a bitch. (So is Isamu—according to a couple of friends.) But back to *The Lark*. Some of the fiction has a kick. There's a story about a love affair conducted in an elevator and another, "The Confessions of a Burglar's Wife," about a marriage that's fueled by the wife's exhilaration as she pushes her thieving husband to pull off more and more audacious robberies in the city's most fashionable homes. "With a languid delight," the wife explains, "I watched my husband as he flitted to and fro among the shadows. How beautifully he burgled! How subtle the play of his slim fingers, and the absolute precision of his movement! I saw that I had never before seen him at his best, and all the resentment I had felt at our difference fled from me, and love resumed full sway again."

If there's some good Dada derangement here and there in the writing, where the craziness really takes off is in the visuals. The Surrealists couldn't improve on "The Lark's Salon: Catalogue Illustré," with European masterworks by Corot, Degas, Manet, Monet, Burne-Jones, and Turner reimagined as crude advertisements composed of bits and pieces of nineteenth-century woodcut illustrations. A Degas becomes a series of four ditsy dancers who look as if they've been rubberstamped in a row. Corot's *Printemps* is two pairs of lovers and three trees—romanticism as a rebus. Then there are the drawings of what Burgess called his Goops, overgrown babies running rampant, putty figures with spherical heads and identical circles for eyes and mouth. "Now you are what I call a GOOP!" he explains,

> A Co-tangent harmonious Loop
> You appear to be facing due South
> But O what have you done with your Mouth?

In one drawing the poor Goop, living in a room with no floor, is forced to clutch the fireplace mantel, feet firmly planted on the bed so as not to drop into a star-strewn black abyss.

The Goops must have kicked off a strong response, because within a couple of years Burgess had published *Goops and How to Be Them: A Manual of Manners for Polite Infants* and *More Goops and How Not to Be Them: A Manual of Manners for Impolite Infants.* Were these books really for kids? Or was Burgess thinking that all adults really are just kids, polite or impolite, it hardly matters? Burgess's time in San Francisco was brief—maybe a decade. He had East Coast yearnings. That's the part that reminds me of me. So he went back East and collaborated with some newspaperman (Will Irwin, apparently a Bay Area buddy) on *The Picaroons*, a not-so-bad series of stories about Barbary Coast dreamers and grifters. All by himself he wrote a wretched novel called *The Heart Line*, about mediums, palm readers, and other assorted San Francisco charlatans. (I gave up halfway through.) During a visit to France he reported on Matisse and the other Paris moderns. What on earth he did for the next thirty or forty years of his life I don't know.

15: LIZ AND DARRYL

Am I turning into some kind of romantic as I sit here in Marin, watching the fog roll in? I can't resist getting a little romantic about Liz and Darryl Smith. They arrived from New York—or maybe I should say they swept in, they were, after all, the glamorous creative couple. They were awfully good-looking, just about perfect as a couple, close to the same height, not too short and not too tall, a sort of postwar Adam and Eve. Darryl, a painter with some good reviews under his belt, wanted you to know that he knew his way around a tennis court and a sailboat. He had a beard, which was unusual in our crowd. It was dark brown, a little dandyish but also casual, carefully but not too carefully trimmed. The blond-haired Liz, sportif as well, had the blandly beautiful profile of some Greek sculpture of Aphrodite. I know this sounds hyperbolic. I can't help it. The two of them—the couple—had a built-in hyperbole.

When I first met Liz she was still painfully serious. After a while she began to regard seriousness as a pain. But we'll get to that. For years she'd worked hard at her painting, only eventually coming to the conclusion that she didn't have what it took. So she decided to change directions. (Change seems to be the constant in Liz's life.) She got herself into a PhD program in the English Department at Berkeley, setting out to write a thesis on the changing image of the artist in Victorian fiction. If it hadn't been for the PhD, I suppose she and Darryl would have never left New York and would still be living in a loft on West 23rd Street, a fantastic deal so they liked to remind us, as if underscoring the sacrifice they had made in coming west. They weren't as short of cash as the rest of us. People whispered that there was money from somebody's family—much, come to think of it, as people have whispered about me behind my back, with smart-alecky remarks about my dad and his liquor store. Darryl and Liz set themselves up in a pretty nice old house in Berkeley, not way up in the hills but not in the real flatlands, either.

They had dinner parties with matching modernist dishes, which Liz admitted with a mixture of embarrassment and pride had been wedding gifts. They frowned on potlucks. They both came from Boston, had known each other since high school. Although their families weren't really old Boston they were prosperous Boston. Darryl's father was a lawyer, Liz's a doctor. They had given the okay to whatever these two were doing. She didn't say it, but I got the impression that New York had turned out to be uncomfortably close to Boston—and Mom and Dad. Their parents—the two couples were great friends—appeared at the Carlyle for long weekends, going to a few plays and insisting on taking Darryl and Liz and some of their friends out to dinner. Darryl's father was perfectly at ease in some old Italian eatery on Houston Street, charming a couple of art school girlfriends of

Liz's, who afterward observed, "We see where Darryl's charm comes from. And he looks just like his dad." This left Liz feeling uneasy.

Darryl had already been noticed a couple of times in *Art News*, a standout in the little cooperative galleries on Ninth Street with his abstract landscapes. He and Liz had studied with Hans Hofmann at his school on Eighth Street and spent a couple of summers at Hofmann's school in Provincetown. They were insiders. They knew all the gossip. We San Franciscans always remind people that Hofmann's first US teaching gig was at Berkeley. I like Hofmann's romantic mystifications, which I've always felt have a kind of Northern California vibe, though it's probably just the vibe of an old-fashioned Bavarian nature lover. The one or two times I met him I found him a discombobulating figure, the German imperiousness mixed up with a disarming informality, the Kantian dicta and the handmade leather sandals from some local beatnik shop. He was armored and disarming, a crackpot genius, more Munich or Marin County than Manhattan, at least so I imagined. Darryl and Liz liked to reminisce about dinners just with him and his wife, Miz, in the Hofmanns' Provincetown house. Miz complained about her husband's infidelities, at least so Liz claimed.

Liz was a confider. Though not with me. We were friendly but not really friends. She told her troubles to Ginny, the kind of masochist who likes to soak up everybody's troubles. I think other people's troubles console Ginny. Anyway, when Ginny began to whisper to me that there was trouble between Liz and Darryl I didn't believe it, not at first. I figured it was just Ginny projecting her own sheepish misery onto others. But I have to hand it to Ginny. She's an insightful misery. She was probably quoting Liz verbatim when she announced in that mournful voice of hers, "Liz says Darryl isn't holding up his end of the bargain." What bargain was that? This was around the time that Darryl had his first show in San Francisco, at Rivka Rubenstein's gallery. Darryl was painting figures, still with his Kandinsky arcs and angles and raucous colors, but now colliding to make recognizable scenes of, god help us, a crowd of guys at an antique car show. Darryl was a car buff. He drove around in an old MG that he was proud to tell you he'd repaired himself. In his paintings the old sports cars were reimagined as some kind of *ballet mécanique*, at least I wouldn't have been surprised if Darryl had been thinking about Léger's experimental film, made sometime in the 1920s. That wasn't necessarily a bad idea, except that Darryl was sentimental about his subject matter. Maybe the problem was that the half-abstracted fellows ogling the cars all had Darryl's beard. Did he think he was an everyman? Although somebody in the *Chronicle* was tickled by the show, *Art News* ran a brief thumbs down review, suggesting that a promising New Yorker had lost his way out west. That was the end of Darryl's career with Rivka Rubenstein, which I guess for Liz meant he wasn't holding up his end of the bargain.

"He's found his level," that's what Ginny told me Liz was saying. "He's making what he figures is enough money to get by, teaching at the Palo Alto Arts Association, where the suburban ladies want to enroll in classes with the genuine New York artist who'll show them how to really paint." I imagined him crinkling his handsome eyes as he wondered what to say about a clotted abstraction by a fidgety blond who was already late to pick up her daughter at nursery school. Meanwhile Liz, who'd been on various teams in college, had turned a part-time grad student job in the sports complex at Berkeley into a full-time gig. She had been on the tennis team in high school and college and now realized she missed running around the court. She was still supposedly working on her PhD, but from what Ginny told me about her comments about "artsy eggheads" I got the impression that she had decided that we didn't really know how to live. I saw her around less and less. She was dressing differently, replacing the blue jeans and plain Jane white blouses with long dresses with flower prints.

Then Liz was gone. In San Francisco she had found the liberation she'd been seeking—and it led her straight out of San Francisco. I say good luck to her. I don't believe in liberation. I'm skeptical about anybody who claims they're blissed out—cheerfully contemplative, belligerently unfettered, just glad to be alive, so they say, and maybe they're telling the truth, though I don't believe a word of it. Christmas cards arrived from Taos, where Liz had bought what I gather was an old motel—more of Mom and Dad's money—and turned it into some kind of spa. The first few Christmas cards she sent were striking accordion fold affairs, silk screen prints that Liz made using the brightest colors. They were abstracted skyscapes—cacti, peaks, sunsets—rather attractive if you like Fauvist fakery. In one corner there was a penciled notation so you knew this was from a limited edition of fifty. I framed one. Put it up in the kitchen. Within a few years her cards were commercial jobs, crummy printing, more of an advertisement for her center—"Stay for a week! Yoga! Massage! In the shadow of ancient American culture! Renew!" The last card I saw was pure trash, a photograph of a couple on matching loungers in swimsuits soaking up the sun. It was barely a holiday card. The real message, in big block letters that overwhelmed the Christmas greetings, was: "Renew your marriage!"

Friends who were driving around the Southwest would give her a call and stop by. Ginny said that when she visited Liz barely gave her the time of day. Left her sitting on the couch in the tiny reception area of the motel for half an hour and then they had a hurried glass of wine. Liz didn't even apologize. According to Ginny the place was tacky, fake cowboy, fake Indian. "She's no longer one of us," Ginny sneered. "And to think Hofmann once said, 'That girl can really paint.' She's become a businesswoman—a down-market Madison Avenue type, selling Southwest renewal. Well, maybe not so down-market. She may be making good money, charging Midwestern matrons top dollar to come to her crappy motel. You wouldn't believe some of the people I saw wandering around that jazzed up motel of hers."

I blame San Francisco for what's become of Liz. She was no genius. I know that. But I always liked her determination. I liked her from the moment I met her. Hell, she was Aphrodite in blue jeans. And when she talked about Hofmann's theories of painting or *The Wings of the Dove* she was Aphrodite playing Athena. I imagined a wise owl (a good-looking owl, Darryl as an owl) resting on her strong, sexy shoulder. But where was she going to go with that? San Francisco—we, yes, we—softened her up. After which she'd had enough of us. She made her exit. As for Darryl, he still appears at parties now and again. The beard has grayed. Still a twinkle in his eye, a drunkard's twinkle is my thought. He lives in a cottage in the flatlands in Berkeley. I'm told you can barely move in the couple of rooms he has, which are crowded with all the unsold semi-abstract paintings of men who look like Darryl admiring old MGs and Jaguars at some Bay Area antique car show. At a party a few years ago I asked him about Liz. "Liz? I think she's doing pretty well."

16: CYNTHIA

I still haven't responded to the letter I received a few weeks ago from Cynthia, Simon's daughter. She wrote a couple of months after Marcia died, just to say how sorry she was, how much Marcia had meant to her, a condolence letter. Now she's writing again, and this time she's looking for something.

Dear Burt,

I'm sorry to be writing again. We only met that one time, for dinner in San Francisco when I was visiting a friend in Menlo Park. But I have to tell you that I'm feeling really angry about everything that's going on. I hope you'll listen to my side of things. Marcia promised to take care of me—to help me get on my feet. She paid off the nursing school loans. That made all the difference. Now I'm set with a really good job at the hospital here in Worcester. And the condo unit I've been renting is up for sale and if I can buy it I'll really be set. Problem is I only have half of the down payment. I need another $1,000. My dad—well, you know, he's impossible. I actually went down to New

York to see him. A friend from nursing school put me up in Queens for a couple of nights. As you are probably aware, Dad (Simon to you) is now living in London with a woman by the name of Suzy Grand. They say she's in the art business, a writer who organizes shows, I'm not really sure. I don't really get their relationship. But then I never really got Dad's relationship with my mom, at least what I can remember of it before he split (I was ten). Frankly, I don't care. Anyway. They were staying at the Algonquin and I called Dad and he agreed to have a drink with me. Fancy hotel! Dad sat in a chair with a really high back, looking obnoxious. And I laid out my problem. And he listened and then it was just, "Darling, I don't have a dime. I'm here with Suzy." That made me mad. I sort of shouted at him, "But you must have something!" All he had to say in return was, "Don't make a scene in here, sweetheart. The little I have, I'll need it if this doesn't work out. For now Suzy's paying all the bills. But if it doesn't work out—well, you don't want me arriving on your doorstep, do you?" And then Suzy appeared, a fat pig in my opinion. Yuck is all I can say. And she sat for a minute and Dad introduced me and Suzy looked me up and down and then it was, "Simon, we're going to be late for dinner." And that was that. So. You're really my only chance. My mom is barely making ends meet. I've been helping her, at least when I can. I know Marcia would have helped. I'm sure of it. Please help me. Sincerely, Cynthia

I'm not sure what Marcia would've done. But I'm beginning to think I'll send Cynthia the money. I find it interesting that she's so sure Marcia would have helped. It's not an insignificant amount of money.

But maybe Cynthia is right. Marcia regarded Cynthia as some kind of lost soul. And Marcia had a fascination, sometimes bordering on obsession, with people and things that were lost or in danger of being lost. A lot of people missed that side of her writing. They never got beyond her braggadocio. But somewhere in her there was an element of regret, a nostalgia for something truer, realer, more authentic. If she hadn't believed in that something I don't think she would have ever bothered to sit down and write. She saw the world of artists and writers and their work—it was the only world she really knew—as a house of mirrors. She loved it and hated it. She wanted to smash the mirror, see what was really there. Some desire to get to the bottom of things might help to explain why she came back from New York when she did. Or why she took up with me again. She had tender feelings for the San Francisco she'd rejected when she headed for New York. When she wrote to Mike that Rome reminded her of San Francisco, she may have been giving us a bigger compliment than she realized at the time.

In Rome, while she was working on *A Night at the Opera*, Carandente introduced Marcia to a man and a woman who had been figures in Roman society since the 1930s, an artist whose lean physique and faded elegance reminded her of Cal Cummings and a princess who still had an important Poussin landscape hanging in her living room. The painter's monochromatic still lifes, Marcia told me, had been much admired in Paris before the war. His name was Signorelli, same as the Renaissance artist. Marcia was never quite clear about the relationship between these two, but they appeared together at some of the rehearsals at the Opera House and took Marcia out to a long lunch at an outrageously elegant restaurant. She loved to describe that luxurious afternoon. Despite their age—Marcia figured the princess was in her early eighties and the painter maybe a decade younger—they seemed to know more than anybody else about new developments in art and literature, not only in Italy but all over Europe and even in the United States. Marcia found this both exhilarating and troubling, wonderful but also unnerving. They struck her as marvelous dinosaurs, refusing their own extinction. "There were moments," Marcia confessed, "when they kind of creeped me out. They seemed almost mummified, so beautifully turned out, so knowledgeable, but unable to accept their expiration date."

Back in the Bay Area, Marcia may have been wondering about her own expiration date. Of course she was only in her forties. But she could see that a lot of what animated her was looking old hat. She hated political theorizing, which she was certain was due for a comeback. She was right about that. And she couldn't figure out how to defend Oscar Wilde's art-for-art's-sake—that was her gospel—against what she saw as the distortion and commercialization of the Irishman's ideas among a younger generation that was turning decadence into a slogan: turn on, tune in, drop out. She was gobsmacked when a photograph of Wilde appeared on a poster for a concert by Jefferson Airplane at the Avalon Ballroom. "The nerve," she announced. "They have no idea what Oscar stood for." There were fresh battles to be fought and she didn't want to take them on. Maybe she knew there was no way she was going to win. She'd been taking potshots at the bohemia of the 1940s and 1950s for so long that she couldn't decide what to think or say about the new San Francisco—which, truth be told, was leaving more than a few of her friends feeling a little like dinosaurs.

It could be that that last night at the Opera House, moments before she collapsed, Marcia was thinking that if she didn't watch out she was going to go the way of Martha Graham. "Like Sarah Bernhardt," as Marcia put it at the time, "on her umpteenth tour, missing a leg or something." Those were her last words. Of course Marcia believed there was something glorious about that kind of crazy exit. Being Sarah Bernhardt wasn't exactly a bummer. Marcia's takedowns always had a celebratory element—a gleefulness. She was an improvisor. Her life was a kind of merry-go-round: Germany, England, San Francisco, New York, Rome, and San Francisco again. She had her fling with Simon. But in the end she sided with his daughter. And damned if she didn't give me another chance. I'm going to send Cynthia the money she's asking for. Spread the wealth around. I can imagine Marcia writing the check and announcing, "Thank god I'm not living in a condo in Worcester."

Coffee House Press began as a small letterpress operation in 1972 and has grown into an internationally renowned nonprofit publisher of literary fiction, essay, poetry, and other work that doesn't fit neatly into genre categories.

LITERATURE
is not the same thing as
PUBLISHING

Funder Acknowledgments

Coffee House Press is an internationally renowned independent book publisher and arts nonprofit based in Minneapolis, MN; through its literary publications, Coffee House acts as a catalyst and connector—between authors and readers, ideas and resources, creativity and community, inspiration and action.

Coffee House Press books are made possible through the generous support of grants and donations from corporations, state and federal grant programs, family foundations, and the many individuals who believe in the transformational power of literature. This activity is made possible by the voters of Minnesota through a Minnesota State Arts Board Operating Support grant, thanks to the legislative appropriation from the Arts and Cultural Heritage Fund. Coffee House also receives major operating support from the Amazon Literary Partnership, and the McKnight Foundation.

Coffee House Press receives additional support from Bookmobile; Dorsey & Whitney LLP; and the Schwab Charitable Fund.

MINNESOTA STATE ARTS BOARD
CLEAN WATER LAND & LEGACY AMENDMENT

amazon literary partnership

McKNIGHT FOUNDATION

The Publisher's Circle of Coffee House Press

Publisher's Circle members make significant contributions to Coffee House Press's annual giving campaign. Understanding that a strong financial base is necessary for the press to meet the challenges and opportunities that arise each year, this group plays a crucial part in the success of Coffee House's mission.

Recent Publisher's Circle members include many anonymous donors, Patricia A. Beithon, Robin Chemers Neustein, Kelli Cloutier, Theodore Cornwell, Jane Dalrymple-Hollo, Jeremy M. Davies, Mary Ebert and Paul Stembler, Kamilah Foreman, Eva Galiber, Bryan Garrett, Roger Hale and Nor Hall, William Hardacker, Randy Hartten and Ron Lotz, Carl and Heidi Horsch, Amy L. Hubbard and Geoffrey J. Kehoe Fund of the St. Paul & Minnesota Foundation, Hyde Family Charitable Fund, Kenneth & Susan Kahn, the Kenneth Koch Literary Estate, Cinda Kornblum, the Lenfestey Family Foundation, Carol and Aaron Mack, Gillian McCain, Mary and Malcolm McDermid, Daniel N. Smith III and Maureen Millea Smith, Vance Opperman, Mr. Pancks' Fund in memory of Graham Kimpton, Alan Polsky, Robin Preble, Ronald Restrepo and Candace S. Baggett, Elizabeth Schnieders, Steve Smith, Jeffrey Sugerman and Sarah Schultz, Paul Thissen, Allyson Tucker, Grant Wood, Margaret Wurtele, Aptara Inc., The Buckley Charitable Fund, and Dorsey and Whitney Foundation.

For more information about the Publisher's Circle and other ways to support Coffee House Press books, authors, and activities, please visit www.coffeehousepress.org/pages/donate or contact us at info@coffeehousepress.org.

JED PERL was the art critic for *The New Republic* for twenty years and a contributing editor to *Vogue* for a decade. He is currently a regular contributor to *The New York Review of Books*. He is the recipient of a Guggenheim Fellowship and the author of numerous books, including *Paris Without End*, *New Art City*, *Authority and Freedom*, and a two-volume biography of Alexander Calder. He lives in New York City. *We Never Called It Frisco* is his first novel.

We Never Called It Frisco was designed by Coffee House Press.
Text is set in Adobe Garamond Pro.